BARRICADES
IN BERLIN

KLAUS NEUKRANTZ

BANNER PRESS
CHICAGO, 1978

𝔇edicated
to the imperishable memory
of the 33, shot by the police
in 𝔅erlin during the days of
𝔐ay 1929

Reprinted in the USA, 1978

**Library of Congress Catalog Card Number: 78-68131
ISBN 0-916650-07-3**

Available from

**BANNER PRESS
PO Box 41722
Chicago, Illinois 60641**

INTRODUCTION

Barricades in Berlin is a stirring novel of armed class warfare. It is the story of the Berlin workers' battle for the right to march through the streets on May Day 1929 and the heroic defense of the Koeslinerstrasse in the heart of the proletarian Wedding district of Berlin. But more, it is a story of the struggle of workers against the power of a capitalist state bent on forcing the working class to bear the brunt of Germany's massive economic crisis and determined to suppress any revolutionary political movement among the workers. The characters in this account are fictionalized, but the novel is based on actual facts and events.

Barricades in Berlin was first published in English in 1933 at the time Adolph Hitler became Chancellor of Germany. It was serialized in the U.S. communist newspaper the *Daily Worker* in the spring of 1933 and had a strong impact on thousands of American workers. It remains today an outstanding example of proletarian literature.

The story line is limited to the few hectic days of the street battles between workers and police in the Wedding and Neükollen districts of Berlin. But the background encompasses the whole period of open and bitter class struggle that raged in Germany in the years between the end of World War I and the triumph of fascism. Less than eleven years before the events described in this book, the German working class had risen up and overthrown the Hohenzollern monarchy of Kaiser Wilhelm II. In November of 1918 red flags flew from the masts of the German fleet after the revolt of the sailors in the port of Kiel. On November 9 hundreds of thousands of workers marched in the streets of Berlin and surrounded the government buildings. Panicky government officials announced the end of the monarchy and the birth of the German Republic. Workers and Soldiers Councils were quickly established throughout the country and for a brief period exercised state power.

But unlike their counterparts in Russia who overthrew the Czar and then the bourgeois government of Kerensky and exercised state power through the Soviets, the German working class was unable to hold onto power in the face of the counter-revolution launched by the capitalists and the landed aristocracy. And whereas the Bolshevik Party was decisive in Russia in carrying through and consolidating the revolution, the role of the Social Democratic Party in Germany was decisive in the defeat of the 1918 revolution and the subsequent setbacks suffered by the working class in the next 15 years. Its role is a central element in the story unfolded in *Barricades in Berlin*.

Founded in the 19th century, the Social Democratic Party called itself Marxist and socialist, and for a time it was a revolutionary party. It had received direct guidance from Marx and Engels and had fought for the interests of the workers against the German ruling classes. But by the eve of World War 1 it had long since abandoned the goal of revolution. In the pre-war period the party was sharply fractured over both the question of reform vs. revolution and the position to take on the impending war. The right wing supported the war and voted for war credits under the slogan "Defend the Fatherland." The Center faction, headed by the likes of Karl Kautsky, took essentially the same position although they sought to find an "internationalist" justification for national chauvinism. Only the left wing of the party, whose most militant forces were headed by Rosa Luxemburg and Karl Liebknecht openly opposed it as a reactionary, imperialist war and called for turning it into a revolutionary civil war. Against the right and the center, the left wing of the Social Democrats threw up the earlier manifestos of European Social Democracy that such a war would be a criminal pitting of worker against worker for the capitalists' profits.

In 1916 Luxemburg and Liebnecht led a split from the

Social Democratic Party and formed the Sparticist League, which in December of 1918 became the Communist Party of Germany. A larger bloc opposed to the war split in 1917 and formed the Independent Social Democratic Party. But the right still remained the majority Social Democratic Party. Both the majority and the Independents made opposition to the Bolshevik revolution a cardinal principle.

The majority Social Democrats held key ministries in the post-war government that was handed the task of signing the armistice and the Treaty of Versailles by the defeated military High Command. When the revolution of 1918 broke out, the majority Social Democrats used all their influence in the working class to try to squash it. Their newspaper *Vorwarts* ran unashamed defenses of the German monarchy. Unable to suppress the revolutionary uprising, however, the Social Democrats were able to successfully co-opt it.

Because of their position as the traditional party of the German working class and the fact that they still held the allegiance of the majority of workers, they were able to obtain the dominant position in the central executive of the Workers and Soldiers Councils and moved forcefully to have the authority of the Councils dissolved into a new National Assembly of all the German parties. The Independent Socialists, in effect, went along with them.

Under the name of a workers' government, the Social Democrat leaders, who were in fact part of the bourgeois state apparatus, carried through the counter-revolution. Representatives of the capitalists and the landed aristocracy soon occupied the key ministries after the elections for the Reichstag in January of 1919.

The defeat of the 1918 revolution was a bloody affair, but it did not end the workers' struggles. The Sparticists led a massive uprising of German workers in Berlin in January of 1919. In April of that year a Bavarian Soviet Republic was declared in Munich in the wake of a popular upheaval. There were large scale workers' uprisings in Central Germany in 1921 and throughout the country in 1923, largely led by the communists. But in each case the workers were defeated by the combined force of the Social Democrats and the military forces of the ruling classes. The Social Democratic military expert Noske recruited and headed up the Free Corps forces from the old imperialist army that put down the workers' uprisings.

In 1929 a Social Democrat, Müller, was German Chancellor. Another Social Democrat, Severing, was Minister of Interior and the Social Democrat Zoergiebel was Police President, or chief of police, of Berlin. While these "socialist" officials let the Nazi Storm troopers demonstrate and rally wherever they dared in Berlin, they directed their force against the communist-led workers.

As May Day 1929 approached, the authorities launched a major effort to silence the workers' demands for radical political and economic changes. May Day demonstrations were prohibited by the police—for the first time in forty years. One reviewer of *Barricades in Berlin* commented at the time of its first U.S. publication: "What not even Kaiser Wilhelm had ventured to do had been done by a stroke of Zoergiebel's pen—Zoergiebel, the Socialist Chief of Police."

This book is written in a militant and openly partisan style from the point of view of the working class. It gives a vivid sense of the fierce struggle against the forces of political and economic reaction waged by the working class in this period. And although it was written over forty years ago it has a liveliness and emotional impact today that is in large part due to the fact that what it describes is a struggle which certainly did not end with the defeat of that May Day battle in Berlin in 1929.

John Krammer
New York, 1978

ABOUT THE AUTHOR

BROUGHT up in a Bourgeois Household—Youth Movement—1914, Volunteer—then four and a half years in the trenches. I met Hugo Haase—the first man from whom I heard something of " Socialism " in the whole of my life, in the Railway Pioneers' Barracks at Königsberg, in the spring of 1919, the day I was demobilised. I understood very little about it at that time, but it sufficed to withhold me from following through my intention of joining one of the East Prussian Detachments of the Volunteer League.* Shortly after I broke with my family in Berlin—I sought to learn, read a great deal in a planless sort of way, attended meetings and lectures, and earned my living as an office worker and by writing mediocre short stories, which were occasionally published here and there. My actual political development really began a few years later when I was an " oppositional " member of the Factory Council in the District Council Office at Kreuzberg (Berlin).† I followed various occupations, worked amongst other things as a hand on a small North Sea vessel, and finally became a Communist as a result of a brief and accidental sojourn with comrades during the period of illegality.‡ From this period onwards the revolutionary working-class took over my education. I was active as an editor for the *Internationale Arbeiterhilfe* (W.I.R.), organised later an Agit-Prop Troup for the " Artists' Aid," which existed at that time, and went with it on tour through the Ruhr Valley, and was finally accepted into the editorial staff of the *Welt am Abend*

* Volunteer League—a secret Fascist " Black Reichswehr " which was in existence at that time.
† The Wiemar Constitution decreed the establishment of Factory Councils in all establishments employing more than thirty workers.
‡ The German Communist Party was illegal from 1923-1925.

ABOUT THE AUTHOR

(Berlin's great workers' evening paper). Followed two years in hospitals and health resorts, which can be laid at the door of the World War. After a lengthy stay in the Soviet Union, I returned to Berlin, and have worked since then as an active Party worker, and revolutionary proletarian writer in the ranks of the working class.

• • • • • •

With regard to the novel which follows, I want to state that neither the personages mentioned therein nor their deeds have been "invented," but have all been taken from the actual events which took place in the Köslinerstrasse during the May days of 1929. Changes have been made only in those cases where there existed the danger of subsequent attack on the persons concerned by the myrmidons of Class Justice. In particular, the police attacks which are described, are taken from the documents of the Investigation Committee, which were placed at my disposal, all of which are vouched for on oath and can be legally verified at any time.

PART I

CHAPTER I

125 HUNDREDWEIGHT OF CEMENT

"NETTELBECKPLATZ . . . !"

The young man peered with a sleepy stare through the glass panes of the tramcar.

"That your newspaper . . . ?" A woman pointed to one lying at his feet. He thrust it into his pocket; in another moment he was outside.

The yellow lights of the gas lamps were reflected on the wet pavement. The shock of wind and rain enlivened him. A loud-speaker boomed from a restaurant at the tram-stop. He was freezing. "A man ought to have an overcoat," he thought, turning up his coat collar. He spat, put his hands in his pockets and walked slowly home.

He hurried from the Pankstrasse, into the dark alley where he lived. The slum shops were already shut. Only the pubs showed signs of life, blurred streaks of light in an empty street illuminated by a few feeble gas jets. Behind the windows of the tall dark houses—mostly curtainless—gleamed here and there a miserable oil lamp. From an open cellar came the warm smell of washing. A few more houses and he was home.

Two women stood at the house door. He nodded briefly at their greeting and vanished in the dark passage. Not till he saw the window of his dwelling from the yard did he pause. "Good . . . Anna is at home," he thought, and reassured he passed his hand over his tired face. This happened every evening as he walked across the yard. He rejoiced at the sight of the bright window. Nothing more.

He felt his way up the few steps of the narrow stairway and opened the door.

" Evening, Anna."

" Evening, Kurt."

He hung his cap on the door hook and dropped into the kitchen chair. The young cement heaver, Kurt Zimmerman was at home.

There was just enough room beside the fireplace in the kitchen for two to sit at the table. Kurt leant his elbows on the table and looked at Anna busying herself with the dishes. He was too tired to speak but it gave him pleasure to sit there and look at her. She handled everything so deftly and quickly.

The warmth of the fire slowly penetrated his damp clothing. The smell of fat and onions was appetising. It occurred to him that he had promised days ago to take Anna to the cinema. " Perhaps we ought to go to-day," he thought sleepily. Anna would like it if only one's bones did not ache so much . . .

. . . The foreman was getting worse and worse. To-morrow the concrete would have to be carried a storey higher. . . .

His eyes closed.

"Now then, lad, eat a bit. . . . Kurt, Kurt,—asleep already ! "

She pushed the plate across and patted his shoulder. As he raised his face to her and passed his hand sleepily over his brow, Anna noticed how pale and tired he was. Since he had started on the building job in Lichtenberg, he came home fagged out every evening. He had been out of work for over six months and he could not stand the pace that was being forced on them there.

"No, no . . ." he smiled wearily, " I am not asleep." He began to eat. Anna sat on the opposite side of the table and looked across. She laughed gently. The spoon was almost swallowed in the broad, heavy palm. When he was tired his heavy awkwardness was emphasized.

Yet Kurt was as good natured as a child. There was only one point on which he could get really very angry, and on that subject she took care not to express her opinion more than was absolutely necessary. She had married Kurt two years ago in the full knowledge that he was in the workers' movement and gave up every free moment to it. There was no use talking to him about it. If there was a meeting, or a job to do, ready as he might be to drop with fatigue, he would insist on carrying on till late at night—then up and away to work again, at half-past five. As if there were not enough unemployed comrades, who could do the job and find time and to spare for sleep. What was the good of it all if his strength was destroyed in the process ? She did not ask much of him otherwise. She was a working woman and knew well enough with how little she must be content. Perhaps he would be off again to-night !

Cautiously she began, " Kurt, have you to go out again later ? "

" No, Anna,—straight to bed this time . . . that is to say," he looked at her hesitatingly, " unless you would rather go to the pictures ? You wanted to—didn't you ? "

" No, lad, that's only an idea of your own," she laughed but she was glad he had asked all the same. It was not a very convincing invitation. They did not always treat each other with so much consideration, but to-night Anna was anxious. She saw how the hard work was pulling him down. But she thought she could rectify all that if she had her way.

Before her marriage, Anna had worked for a long time in a factory, and the tender, dreamy girl had gone through a hard school. Anna knew what life meant.

Kurt pushed back his plate with a yawn : " Is there another drop of coffee ? "

" To-morrow, Kurt. Go to bed now, your night is over at half-past five."

He got up and stretched. What a dog's life ! Work, feed, sleep ! A good thing for once that there was no meeting to-night. Besides it was only at night he could see the kid.

Slowly he began to undress.

" Anna, I shall have to put my old jacket on to-morrow. Look, this has gone at the shoulders again."

He threw the clothes on a chair, old things much patched and darned.

In his bare feet he groped his way across the narrow passage into the bedroom, the only other room apart from the kitchen they possessed. There was a candle on a chair beside the bed, but not much for its light to shine on. They had not yet been able to buy proper window curtains even. Every night Anna took the old red bed cover and hung it in front of the window. In his wife's bed the kid was asleep.

Kurt felt frozen in bed. The bed clothes smelt damp like the whole dwelling, with its eternal damp patches on the wall.

Lying on his back, his bones ached merely from the pressure of his weight. It had been a devil of a job again to-day . . . he had carried 125 hundredweight of concrete up the ladder into the building . . . as long as one did not get ill . . . then the job's gone . . . next Wednesday they were not going to work . . . that's good . . . to-morrow there's a meeting . . . if only that darned wireless above would shut up.

Anna carefully wound the alarm and put the clock on the chair. He seemed to recover consciousness for a moment when Anna bent over his face to put out the light.

He felt that her skin was soft and warm.

CHAPTER II

THE street slept. Its few dim lamps only served to increase its desolate appearance. The last pubs were closed. From somewhere came the rattling sound of a wooden blind being let down. A startled cat ran across the street and vanished through the broken pane of a cellar window. Then everything was quiet.

The night wind brought from the railway bridge on the Nettelbeckplatz, the hollow, long-drawn-out rumble of the last trains. A few glimmers of light behind curtained windows, marked the sombre looming faces of the tenements. One after another they were extinguished. In the stony abysses of the Wedding district night comes early. The worker's night is short.

The only sound in the street came from the hob-nailed boots of the police patrols passing at regular intervals. Always three together.

Between black walls and narrow yards flowed the turbid waters of the Panke. A sewer for factory waste in which the children bathed in the summer—even the stars on this cold, cloudless April night were not reflected in it.

The cramped rooms contained several people apiece. A fetid air enveloped the faces of the sleepers. Stairs, passages, bedrooms, yards—all intolerably crowded together, the smell of humanity permeating walls, cracks, partitions ; a compost of tenants, sub-tenants, lodgers— and children, the curse of the street ! Hardly a child had a bed to itself. In all great, hungry Berlin nowhere else was such poverty to be found—and so many children.

Homeless derelicts huddled undisturbed on the stairs.

15

Strange, human bundles, these also slept and had their short, painful dreams, their anxieties and longings . . .

In one of the yards the silence was broken rhythmically by the hacking cough of a consumptive. Behind the red curtains of a fourth-floor window, a light went out. In the narrow kitchen lay not only old mother Johannsen who never managed to get to sleep until morning, but also the lodger, a young metal worker. In the heavy atmosphere of the narrow space, he felt the hot mouth of the girl who was sleeping with him. Behind the wall a wireless set still played dance music.

A windowpane clattered in the yard. There was the shout of a drunken man, and several hundred people living in the different blocks heard it and thought: " Franz is drunk again ! "

It is all too narrow . . . a man must have some air . . . a prisoned creature always hurting itself bashing against the other man and the walls . . . must have air. Make room ! Make room there ! Willi, give us another Schnappes . . . that loosens the lumps in your throat, and makes everything bright. . . . And then Franz comes home and wants to break things up.

Men slept and dreamt in the night. Not such dreams as those have who rest in big clean bedrooms. Short torturing dreams, overcast by the fixed repulsive faces of pawnbrokers, the charity organisation officials, Labour Exchange bullies, the Poor Law doctor, the Workhouse porter. . . . Threatening, hostile faces, grotesques, ghostly distorted shreds of a brutal reality still haunt the night in dreams that bring sweat to the bodies of the sleepers . . . dreams of ever swifter conveyors . . . of roaring, crushing steam hammers, of the nerve-destroying rhythm of automatic stamping machines, of falling masses of concrete. Women cry out in their sleep because their bodies cannot forget a torture long since scarred over. Dreams of youths in whom life has yet been fully burnt out, miserable, petty, bourgeois longings . . . a white-washed dwelling-room with big yellow sunflowers . . . a swing for little girls on Sundays . . . glowing red paper lanterns on a summer

evening . . . children dream of new shoes, of the warm
fire in the schoolroom, of the apples sold by the old apple-
woman outside. And while the children dream, bugs fall
from the stained ceilings on their soft warm skin.

Resounding knocks sound on a door. In three, or four
of the bedrooms the heavy thumping beats like a fist in
the brain of sleepers. In the few seconds between sub-
conscious perception of the noise and conscious hearing
crowd terrifying dreams. Dreams of the court bailiff
coming for eviction, of the police coming to search the
house, of the rent-collector with a threatening demand for
arrears.

Damp with sweat, the sleeper wakes, his dreams dissi-
pated by a new burst of knocking.

"Who is that . . . ? "

" Open the door, Paul . . . I've forgotten my key."

It is only the lodger. In three or four bedrooms, sleepers
fall back on their pillows relieved.

A long poison draught of night.

.   .   .   .   .   .

In big light rooms of the bourgeois quarter, open windows
inhale the tranquil air of the gardens. Children are asleep
in white beds. Every evening they pray :

> Tired I go now to my rest.
> Let my eyes to sleep be pressed.
> Heavenly Father, let your eyes
> Guard my bed till I arise.

They then go to sleep, and dream of God, the Father with
the long white beard, of night with her train of stars, of
snow-white horses that carry them on wings over the
nocturnal city, and of their new dolls, named Ruth and
Rose, dressed in silk. . . .

In the alley of Wedding, the yards are so close to each
other that little Haidi, when she stands at the window in
the evening cannot see the stars. In the Wedding alleys,
night's train of stars has been transformed into an oppres-
sive blanket, half-suffocating the children. In the alleys

of Wedding, the grown-ups do not teach children to fold
their hands, but show them how to clench fists and say,
" RED FRONT ! "

And many dreamed of this in the red alley, on this night,
which was separated by four times twenty-four hours from
the 1st of May.

At five o'clock the first steps sound on the stairs, and men
walk shivering, with bundles under their arms across the
still dark yard.   From Wedding railway station, early
trains full of silent, sleepy workers, set out for the
industrial quarters of Siemensstadt, Rummelsburg and
Reinickendorf . . .

CHAPTER III

THE same morning precisely at ten o'clock, a fat little man with a black portfolio under his arm knocked at the door on the fourth floor of number three. There was no answering sound. He knocked again, harder and louder.

On the opposite side of the landing the door opened an inch or two, and through the crack an old woman eyed suspiciously the man with the portfolio.

" What do you want with them . . . ? "

The little man turned round. " Could you tell me whether Mrs. Krüger has gone out ? "

The old woman looked the man silently up and down, then shut the door with an angry bang. He gave a nervous start. " Unpleasant people here . . ."

He turned once more to the closed door on the other side of the dark, dirty landing.

A typewritten notice with an official stamp at the foot, had been stuck on one of the doorposts. The fat man knocked again very loud. " Mrs. Krüger, if you don't open the door yourself, I shall have the lock forced," he shouted with his mouth at the keyhole.

In the dwelling behind the door, a child began to cry. From below the creak of a door was heard, and someone came slowly up the stairs. It was a worker who stopped when he saw the fat man.

" Ho, ho . . . it's you ! Don't kick up such a row, my wife is ill ! " he said in a surly tone and went downstairs again. Presently the fat man heard him running across the yard.

The fat man became more and more uncomfortable. If he could only get into the room without using force ! It seemed so dangerous to break the door. Good God ! one was only an official and had to do what one was told ! Groping in the portfolio his hand came on the packet containing his breakfast which was always carefully wrapped up for him by his wife so that it should not make his papers greasy.

He spoke cautiously through the keyhole. " Now, Mrs. Krüger, open the door, I will see what can be done ! "

Without his having heard a step, the door was suddenly thrown open so violently that he jumped back from his bent position in terror.

" What do you want ? . . . Keep out of here. . . . Fetch the police if you want to ! "

In the narrow gloomy entrance stood a young woman carrying a crying child wrapped in a torn brown cloth. In her fear she shrieked in such a penetrating voice that it could be heard right across the yard.

" Well ! I know her type all right," reflected the fat man. When he saw that the woman was all alone in the house he soon recovered his composure. Hastily he put his foot between the door and the wall and with his massive bulk he pushed the little pale woman aside.

" Mrs. Krüger, I must point out that you must not render yourself guilty of resistance to the State authority. " In spite of the fact that the woman was almost out of her senses from anxiety and excitement and did not take in a word he was saying, he recited his official formula : " Since in spite of repeated demands you have not paid the arrears of rent due from you, to the amount of 47 marks, and since the Poor Law office refuses to pay the rent in addition to the current weekly relief of 8 marks allowed to you, you have been directed to evacuate this dwelling by 10 a.m. this morning. Since you have not acceded to this demand, it is my duty to carry out the eviction order against you. Put your things together immediately.   There is a cart below to take your furniture to the Workhouse. I have not much time."

He turned round without paying further attention to the woman and kicked back the door of the only room the dwelling boasted. There was not much to be cleared out ! It is remarkable, reflected the fat man as he looked round at the bare room, that these houses look fairly respectable from the outside. One would never imagine that there could be such misery here. These people haven't even got a bed ! Only children, and nothing to eat.

A low moaning aroused his attention. On an old mattress in the middle of the floor lay a little fair-haired girl wrapped in an old bed cover. The prominent cheek bones standing out from her sunken, colourless face produced a quite unnatural effect. From her thin, almost fleshless neck, the larynx projected under the bloodless skin.

" Terrible that such a thing can go on living," muttered the fat one with a reproachful shake of the head. He was really unpleasantly affected. Oh ! what misery !

He strode over to the window to call to his furniture removers below. He wanted to get the eviction over as quickly as possible. He opened the window and leaned out.

What the deuce was happening ?

He saw with amazement that the appearance of the yard had altered. First it had been empty : now it was full of excited women, vigorously addressing his porters. The latter did not appear to be opposing them very much. Some of the women were watching the window when his head emerged.

" That's the fellow."

Hundreds of faces looked up at him.

" Out with the swine . . . get away from the window . . . bloody jailer . . . skunk ! "

" He ought to be ashamed to take on such a job ! "

He stepped back in alarm. Good God ! the whole building was in an uproar . . . ! What did the people want of him ? Perhaps it would have been better if he had brought a policeman—that's what one gets for being good natured !

He looked about in indecision. The sick child at his

feet still moaned quietly ; she probably had high fever ;
perhaps was hardly conscious. . . .

"Chuck the bastard out."

He gave a start, and hearing, quite close, the long-
drawn screech of the women, he ducked involuntarily.
Perhaps they will throw stones ? If only he were out
of this. But now it was impossible for him to pass
through the crowd. He heard footsteps coming up the
steps.

"They are coming ! " he whispered to himself.

The footsteps came ever nearer. Many pushing, threatening footsteps. From the landing where the sobbing woman
was standing with her child came a deep, masculine voice :
"Never mind, Mrs. Krüger, don't be afraid. Just let us
pass through."

The door was opened. The fat man clutching his portfolio stood trembling near the window. His short flabby
neck was swollen, his veins stood out like red bands, and
his mouth was half open with excitement.

He was faced by a broad shouldered worker, about
thirty-five, but with hair already going grey. The worker
turned towards the sick girl. Something was passing in his
expressionless face. His thin lips contracted. The three
furniture removers of the court bailiff followed him into
the room.

Something about the grave countenance facing him
seemed to pacify the fat man. This was a leader ; he
evidently possessed authority here. Bowing slightly the
functionary took a step towards him.

"Bendovsky is my name . . . Bendovsky," he repeated
politely. "Just listen to me, sir . . . I am awfully sorry
and upset myself . . . especially seeing the child here . . .
no . . . terrible . . . What times we live in ! But let me
try and convince you please that I have no other course."
He fumbled excitedly in his portfolio and pulled out a
typewritten sheet of paper.

The worker cut him short with a quick movement of
his hand. "All very well . . . you know what you are doing
. . . a man who accepts such jobs from scoundrels, must

be one himself ! " He spoke without looking at the fat man, then turned to the porters behind him :

" But you—you are proletarians, the same as us. They offer you a few pence and make you into enemies of your own class. Look round, comrades. The man has been unemployed for two years. He is a consumptive and so gets no dole. The girl has been ill for over a year. The four people living here get every month 32 marks from the Public Assistance Committee, and a bottle of lysol from the Consumptive Department. Two months ago they pumped the lysol out of the man's stomach. That almost finished him. He tries to earn a few pence in the market. This hole costs him 25 marks a month, and they live on the remaining 7 marks which includes all luxuries and summer holidays. Now let's see whether you still have the courage to carry them rags and sticks and put the sick child in the street. Try,—and we'll show you ! " Without looking round he turned, and went out of the room.

There was perfect silence for a moment. The fat man looked at the three workers with a mistrustful, leering glance. One of them raised his head and said quite loudly : " No . . . I won't do it ! We should be rats. Do it yourself—sir."

The other two nodded, looked at the now motionless child and disappeared in the passage.

Once more the fat one was alone with the child. He f lt so helpless—no way out. He was puzzled by this refusal of the workers. It was preposterous. These men had been hired, paid a good wage . . . and now they won't do it—— !

The Court Bailiff Bendovsky was too practical a man to waste too much time with problems he could not understand. He put his bowler hat firmly on his bald head. On the landing he found the workers who had been in the room.

" Oh . . . Sir . . . Sir . . . excuse me. . . . I'm afraid I don't know your name. . . . Perhaps you will be so kind as to see that I can leave this house in safety ? "

He overflowed with politeness. " Perhaps I can have

your attention for a few moments, to discuss the other
evictions in the street. . . . What am I to do now ? " He
took out a whole bundle of eviction orders from his
portfolio.

" You need have no fear ! " the worker said calmly, " no
one will harm you." He purposely made as if he had not
heard the statement about the other evictions. " They
seem to have a good many things in store for us yet," he
thought, and whistled softly between his teeth.

The women on the stairs greeted the three workers with
loud cheers. One of them brought out a big pot of coffee
and three well-buttered slices of bread. They were all
laughing and gabbling. Nervous tension and excitement
had given place to happiness.

For the time being at any rate, the alley—through the
solidarity of the three workers—had beaten the " bums."
The porter told them that they were unemployed, that
this work had been given them by arrangement with the
Trade Union, and that they had not had the faintest idea
what type of work it was to be.

Someone put a few cigarettes into their pockets. After
all the three were unemployed, and the loss of a few marks
meant no small thing to them. In the circumstances, and
since there had been " refusal to carry out the work
supplied " they would most likely lose their unemployment-
benefit. This affair had an important meaning for many
standing on the stairs. There was more than one amongst
them who for many days had had an eviction order lying
on the kitchen table. Now they must all unite and
organise.

" Here he is ! " A woman pointed upstairs, where the
fat man stood on the landing, unable to pluck up sufficient courage to come down the densely packed steps.

As soon as he was observed, the excitement broke out
afresh. There were loud threats.

" Comrades, no nonsense . . . let him pass in peace !
The broad-shouldered worker stood behind the fat man.
The working women stood aside. The bailiff not daring to
raise his eyes, and, pressing his portfolio tightly to his side,

ran quickly down the steps, amidst an icy silence. His terror would have been still greater had he seen the eyes that followed him. But when he ran, with his short quick strides across the yard, a broken old flower pot fell just behind him. In the passages the children whistled after him through their fingers.

Only when he reached the Nettelbeckplatz, and saw the glittering helmet of the policeman, did his deadly terror disappear. He only now noticed that he was running. What if anyone had seen him ?

. . . . . .

The broad-shouldered worker with his young head and his grey hairs, went slowly up the stairs to his flat in No. 3. He had become very thoughtful. On the enamel plate of the door behind which he disappeared was written HERMAN SÜDERUPP. He was the political leader of the Communist street cell.

CHAPTER IV

"THE RED NIGHTINGALE"

"HI . . . Fritzi, get hold of her."

"Keep that door shut . . . !"

"Ha . . . ha . . . look, she's got a hole in her stocking. . . ."

"Now I'll get her. . . . Damn the bitch ! She scratched me. . . . To hell with her ! "

The boy glared at the red mark on his hand. . . . "The bitch . . . scratches like a cat ! " His chums roared with laughter.

"You are rotters, all of you," the girl shrieked breathlessly. It was plain that she was genuinely angry.

"Oh ! don't put on airs . . . Grete. Afraid you'd lose your beauty ? " exclaimed a snub-nosed young fellow in an open shirt, as he spat eloquently on the floor.

"As soon as one has a bit of fun with a woman, she gets huffy."

The girl turned on him excitedly, " You fellows think that we are only here to muck about with. Whenever Otto isn't here you go off your dots and think of nothing but pawing. . . . How is it that it all used to be so different with young chaps in Wedding. Because once we had political work to do, and those who wanted to fool about were thrown out till they had cooled off."

"Look at the little 'un, she's warming up."

"You—Grete ! "

"Don't you dare touch me—or——"

"Calm down, Grete, and don't be huffy. I only wanted to say that you are quite right, we've only been fooling around," said Fritz, who had soon forgotten his scratch. He was really sorry he had handled her so roughly. The other boys muttered to themselves and looked embarrassed.

Nearly every evening the youth of the Köslin quarter met in the " Red Nightingale."

To-night as usual something was going on in every one of the noisy, smoke-filled rooms. The workers of the alley gave the " Red Nightingale " a distinct political atmosphere, something not to be found in usual pubs. This one was more like a Red workers' club than anything else. Everybody knew everybody else, and strange faces were rarely seen. Strangers were met with suspicion.

Once some C.I.D. men had sat down at a table in here, and taken out a copy of the *Rote Fahne* from their pockets, in order to appear innocent. They were not known personally in Köslin, but the workers only needed to see how they sat down, how they took up their glasses of beer. . . . It was as if their very smell had given them away from the moment they came in and said " Good evening " in so conciliatory a tone. These fools really thought they could sit down peacefully in the " Red Nightingale " and gather information. They found themselves outside in the fresh air before they had warmed their seats. Since then the " splits " had left the place in peace. Whoever did not belong there had to remain outside !

Several Communist dailies and illustrated papers, neatly clipped in holders, hung on the walls. Above were large notice boards with photographs belonging to the Workers' Sports Clubs which met here. On one side, was a counter with a case for sausages ; behind it a large cupboard with bright mirrors containing beer and glasses, cigarettes, bottles of spirits, etc. On a square cardboard notice was written :

GOOD NON-ALCOHOLIC DRINKS,
10 PFENNIGS A GLASS.

Behind the counter stood the owner of the " Red Nightingale," Black Willi. He was a quiet, good-natured man, who sometimes gave credit up to fairly large sums to his unemployed customers, making the entry in his greasy black book.

But the " Red Nightingale " was no boozing den ! If you had no money, or did not feel like a drink, you just sat there without one, took part in any discussion that might be going on, or else played cards or chess. Of course you were not at the Ritz ; it was the workers' meeting place in the " Red Alley."

The roomy passage leading to the small hall at the back of the house was the meeting place of the youngsters, nearly all of whom were dressed in the grey uniform of the Red Front Fighters' League, and the Jungsturm. A discussion was in full swing, Otto, the leader of the Youth section, had arrived.

" Comrades, nobody can hear if you shout like that." A young man, still in his overalls, roared above the din. Fritz turned on him.

" But, Otto—it's ridiculous. How can he prohibit the 1st of May, after the Transport Workers have twice voted unanimously for celebrating it ? If the trains stop, how can there be work in Berlin ? " His comrades burst out into loud roars of laughter.

" Ha, ha, Fritz, aren't you clever, Fritzi ! Perhaps the Police President hasn't heard of it yet ! " Roars of laughter.

" Order, Comrades," Otto called out in a loud voice. " Don't just laugh at Fritzi in that silly way. He is partly right. If the trains don't run on Wednesday, that would be a victory for us. That gives a different appearance to the town, and the respectable people will notice it first thing in the morning that something is on. But of course the ban on the demonstration will not depend on that. Here, let me show you how many of the Social Democratic workers still cling to the illusion that ' Comrade ' the Police President will still change his mind. Just listen to this.'

He took a newspaper from his pocket and unfolding it, began to read : " Is Comrade Zörgiebel quite unaware of the fact that others beside Communists will demonstrate on the 1st of May ; faithful old Party comrades of ours, who will not allow anyone to take away their right to demonstrate on May Day ? Is he not conscious of the fact that his action means a heavy blow to the forty years old

May Day tradition of our Party ? Isn't our comrade concerned a little about lining-up with Bulgaria and Jugo Slavia—the countries where the white terror reigns ? Doesn't Comrade Zörgiebel see any other way than the despotic way . . . ? "

His audience attended closely to the reading. Some workers came from the front room and stood in the doorway. Otto now held the paper up high, so that all could see it.

" And who writes that ? The Social Democratic paper in Plauen ! "

Fritzi looked round triumphantly. " There you are, what did I say ? " Otto laughed good humouredly.

" One moment, Fritzi, not quite so fast. Of course many good workers belonging to the Social Democratic Party think like that ! But we should be fools to imagine that the ' Comrade Police President ' will take any notice of them. Damned if he will ! These ' Left ' S.P.D. papers write like that because many of their readers think the ban a dirty trick. Right ! but in doing so they keep the opposition within their own ranks. This is the job of the ' left ' S.P.D. We shall see what these ' lefts ' will do on Wednesday, whether as ' good Party comrades,' they will allow their right to hold demonstrations to be ' taken away from ' them by their ' comrades ' or not ! "

" We'll put Kunstler* in the middle," a worker called out and laughed.

" Comrades," Otto continued, " The point is that at this moment neither the S.P.D. nor the Government can tolerate a mass demonstration of a Communist revolutionary character in the streets. That is the reason for the ban, which will certainly not be lifted."

Even now, Fritzi was not quite convinced ; though all the rest agreed with Otto.

It surely meant something if a Social Democratic paper could write like that ! Fritzi had an inner conviction that the ban on the demonstration would be lifted before May Day. He decided to speak to Comrade Hermann the political leader of the Party cell about it. The street cell

* Berlin Secretary to the S.P.D.

had a meeting to-night at the "Nightingale." Perhaps Hermann would have something fresh.

The door was suddenly pushed open, and a girl breathlessly thrust her way through the crowd. On her grey coat she wore the badge of the Young Communist League.

"Otto . . ." she shouted from the door, "In the Badstrasse the Nazis attacked three of us !"

"Quick to the rescue."

Alarms of this kind had become frequent of late. Apparently the Nazis were working according to definite plan with the object of terrorising Red Wedding through attacks on individual workers.

.   .   .   .   .   .

In the empty room Black Willi went slowly to the rear and opened the window.

"They smoke like chimneys," he mumbled, emptying the ashtrays, and, pushing a few chairs into their places.

In the front room were a few elderly workers, and among them old Hubner, who despite his sixty-eight years, was active in the Party cell. He wore a clean blue cap over his white hair. Like many old people his skin which lay in innumerable wrinkles grew daily whiter and more transparent—perhaps because he was eating less and less. The son he lived with had been out of work for almost a year. The old man gave most of his food to his four little grandchildren. Children find it more difficult to starve than old people. He placed his bony hands, knotted with blue veins, on the handle of his stick and looked across at the landlord.

"Willi. What do you think about this business ?"

Black Willi was wiping the counter with a cloth. He waited a few seconds. You were never sure, with old Father Hubner, whether he intended to continue or not.

"Well, Father Hubner," he replied at last, "that's not easy to say. Only I think that if blood flows next Wednesday it will suit the book of those gentlemen at the top. Otherwise why should they have imposed the ban ?"

The old man shook his head. "No, no, Willi, I still cannot believe it. I am an old man, and I have celebrated

every May Day for over forty years, ever since I became an organised worker I have gone on the streets. Willi, I can remember how in 1890 we demonstrated for the first time on May Day with red carnations and ties here in Berlin, outside near the Landsberger Tor. It was such a scare for them that they went and founded the Federation of Berlin Metal Employers, to protect themselves against the May Day demonstrations. These gave the police 3,000 marks for ' services rendered,' because they drew their swords against us,—but it didn't help them any. . . ."

He was silent for a moment as if concentrating on a problem. " Willi . . . do you think . . . that after Wednesday money will be given to the Berlin Police President for services rendered, too ? "

And suddenly Father Hubner spat—a thing he otherwise would never do—spat into the middle of the room. His fleshless, trembling fingers pressed the handle of the stick until the kunckles were white.

" But I won't, Willi, I won't stay at home," he exclaimed with a strangely altered voice. Then he rose heavily, threw two coins on to the table, and limped out without another word.

" Christ ! " the old chap was in a wax. Black Willi looked after him in amazement, he had never seen the old fellow like that before. Father Hubner had decided to leave the Social Democratic Party and join the Communist Party after the bloody suppression of the rising in Central Germany in 1921. After all it was no trifle to have been a member of a Party for over thirty years, the Party which to-day provided the man who prohibits the 1st of May celebrations with police terrorism. Angrily he threw the cloth under the counter. " Damned pigs . . . ! " he muttered, and slouched behind in order to prepare the small hall for the meeting.

CHAPTER V

THE 145TH STREET CELL

EIGHT O'CLOCK. Gradually, one after another, they came through the door and went towards the small hall. They were mostly mature working men and women in shabby, worn-out clothes. They knew and greeted each other, asking after the sick child, the morning's evictions, and all the rest. People knew about each other's worries here.

The door was opened again.

" RED FRONT ! " Hermann entered with a packet of leaflets under his arm.

" Well, Hermann, anything new ? "

The habitual question these days ! Too much was in the air. At the Labour Exchanges, in the factories, on the streets, in the trams and shops, everywhere fantastic rumours. Agent-provocateurs, friends, enemies—who could tell ? They say that the army will be brought into action on Wednesday. The Police President has issued a special decree about street fighting. The ban will be definitely lifted for the 1st of May. Reichsbanner and the Stahlhelm have been put into police uniforms—and so on, endlessly. The bourgeois papers, *Tempo*, and the evening edition of *Vorwärts* are bombarding Berlin with inflammatory headlines. Which are facts ? Which are lies ?

Hermann placed his leaflets on the table.

" Comrades—don't be so nervous ! Here is the news. The very latest is that Brolat (Trade Union Official) has prohibited the Transport Workers from demonstrating on the 1st of May ! "

" What ? "

" That isn't true ! "

32

" If the evening edition of *Vorwärts* says so it ought to be true," Hermann replied dryly.

" The scoundrel, shame on him, and he wants to be Mayor of Wedding."

At once the room was filled with excited discussion.

So that's what they want to do ! and what will Transport workers say to this ? Since when have the workers been dictated to, as to whether they should celebrate the 1st of May or not ? Calls himself Social Democrat—hell of a Socialist ! Why do S.P.D. mandarins occupy directors' chairs in Municipal enterprises ? If the Transport workers stopped work that would put the tin hat on everything, therefore Brolat must intervene and give the assistance of the Trade Union Bosses in order to prevent the traffic workers stopping work on the 1st of May, as they had decided. It was sheer defiance of the result of the ballot. The whole thing plain as a pikestaff !

Some of the young Communists returned. The Nazis had fled. Fritzi pushed his way through the crowd, his face flushed with excitement. Hermann greeted him kindly. He knew the enthusiastic little comrade, who came to him often when he was puzzled about something.

" Good evening, Comrade Hermann. Well, what do you think ? Don't you agree that the ban will be lifted ? Otto has a Social Democratic paper which is thoroughly annoyed with their ' Comrade Zörgiebel.' "

Herman's grey eyes laughed mockingly. " You silly boy ! Just wait and you'll see on Wednesday his Excellency the President will go for a walk with a red carnation fixed to his top hat, whistling the International."

Fritzi stood snubbed, among the laughing workers. Suddenly Grete pushed past him, and stopped with angry face, in front of Hermann.

" If we wanted to get such a silly answer, it wasn't necessary to ask you. You want to be a political leader, and talk like a monkey to a young comrade. Then you swear at the young Communists for lack of political activity. But dare to ask you a question, and out come your stupid jokes ! " She turned her back, leaving

C

Hermann dumbfounded, and drew Fritzi out of the room.

" Don't let it bother you, Fritzi. Hermann won't forget what I told him ! "

They thought they heard Hermann calling after them, " Go to hell ! " as they went home across the dark, rainy street.

Silence reigned in the little hall when Hermann tapped his glass with his pencil. Everyone knew that this evening important things would be discussed. Next to the leader of the cell sat a young man of about thirty, keenly scrutinising the faces of the workers in front of him. The District Committee had sent him, its representative, to lead off the discussion. On the wall above the table hung three large pictures of Lenin, Liebknecht and Rosa Luxemburg ; the Liebknecht and the Rosa Luxemburg drawn in charcoal by a young comrade. The restricted platform was garnished with the chests and cupboards of the Workers' Sports Clubs. Dusty garlands, made of now faded tissue paper, festooned the blackened ceiling and were in strange contrast with the serious and businesslike conduct of the meeting. On a piece of cardboard above the piano was a hand-written notice :

SUNDAY EVENING DANCE.
ENTRANCE FREE.

There were now about forty-five men and women present —the street cell of the Köslin quarter. Some of the men— most of them were still in working clothes—had their tool-bags with them. The faces, set and colourless, bore the common imprint of years of heavy labour, and daily anxieties : the uniform of the oppressed class.

Hermann rose.

" Comrades, the aggregate meeting is opened. The first point on the Agenda is the Trade Unions and the 1st of May. The second point, preparatory work for the 1st of May. Before calling upon the comrade from the district to speak, I wish to ask group leaders and treasurers to stay for a few minutes after the meeting is over. No one may leave before the end. And now, Comrade delegate——"

All faces turned towards the young comrade, who had risen. His right hand covered some written notes and newspaper cuttings lying on the table.

"Comrades, I will only speak for a little while, so that we can have a thorough discussion afterwards."

His speech at first was unemphatic but clear, and every word was easily understood. He bent forward slightly, as if to come nearer to the workers before him. With one hand he adjusted his spectacles, a movement which he repeated frequently in the course of his speech.

"If we examine the events of the last weeks, we find far more clearly than in the last few years two implacable class forces bitterly opposed to one another, facing each other with all sharpness. The new emphasis began with the factory council elections in the spring of this year! Throughout Germany they signified an incontestable victory for the Communist Party, and the Revolutionary Trade Union Opposition. In all the large factories, in the mines and smelting works of the Ruhr area, at Siemens, the A.E.G., in the Berlin Transport Co., in the Leuna works, in the chemical hells of Associated Chemical Combine Industry and, in the same way, in the big shipbuilding yards Blohm and Voss in Hamburg, the Germania Dockyard in Kiel, everywhere we gained a decisive victory, and the reformists suffered a decisive defeat."

He paused for a moment, and looked towards the door where someone had come in noisily. Then he continued : "Comrades, there is a direct connection between these factory council elections, and the ban on the May Day demonstrations." He passed his hand through the air in a straight line. "For once a bourgois paper hit the nail on the head when it wrote recently : 'The *Rote Fahne* is right in considering hellish fear to be the mother of Comrade Zörgiebel's courage.'"

"That's right," a woman called out loudly from the back of the hall. When her neighbours turned round, she tried to hide her embarrassment by pretending to adjust her shawl.

" That's right," she muttered and fidgeted. Herman tapped his glass.

" In this connection we must see what rôle the Trade Union leaders are playing to-day in the camp of the enemies of the working-class. After the International Workers' Congress in Paris in 1889 had decided to celebrate the 1st of May as the fighting day of the working-class, the Berlin Trade Unions were the first to start active propaganda for the celebration of May Day in 1890. Towards the end of March a manifesto signed by the most varied Trade Union branches, appeared in the *Volks Tribune* and *Volksblat,* headed ' What is to happen on May the 1st ? '—In all industrial cities it was planned to celebrate May Day as a holiday of the working-class under the slogan ' Fight for the eight-hour day,' by ceasing work and organising street demonstrations.

" Despite strong opposition the workers have stood by their May Day ever since. The very first May Day celebra tion was followed by an intense struggle in the Berlin metal industry. All moulders were locked out. They put forward their own demands ' Shorter working day, and a minimum wage.' In 1896 the Trade Unions fought the employers for twenty-six weeks as a result of the 1st of May. Two years previously, the Berlin Trade Unions had started the well-known beer boycott on the 1st of May in order to enforce their demands. You see, comrades, the 1st of May in those days was always a fighting-day and a day of celebration for the Trade Unions, especially in Berlin. "

He paused, took a step backward, and raised his voice.

" As early as 1903, Cohn, whom you know very well, said openly at the Congress of Metal Workers, that sooner or later, all the business of May Day celebrations would have to be done away with. In the subsequent discussion which lasted for years the right-wing reformist leaders came out more and more openly against the stopping of work on May the 1st. Again and again Rosa Luxemburg, in her bitter struggle against revisionism within the Social Democratic Party, took the 1st of May as her example of the disastrous reformist deviations of the Trade Union leadership. It was no accident that these discussions coincided with the hotly-debated question of the General Strike. For ten years, the two fronts were diverging. Finally, after the proletariat had celebrated May Day thirty-four times as the fighting-day of the working-class, the day came when Karl Liebknecht thundered ' Down with the War—Peoples of the World Arise ! ' and two parties faced each other as implacable foes in the frenzy of the World War.

" After the War, May Day celebrations were taken for granted. Were the workers to lose under a Republic what they had forced from a Kaiser ? But what in fact happened ? The Social Democratic Party had become an important part of the State Machine and the capitalist Republic. Just as at the beginning of the political up-heavals the S.P.D. with Noske and the Black Reichswehr drowned the workers' rising in blood, the same S.P.D., in the period of reconstruction of German industry undertook the policeman's job of keeping down the working masses, since only at their expense was the stabilisation of the position of the employers possible. If we survey the entire post-War development, even an S.P.D. worker will have to admit that in every single decisive situation the capitalists have always left it to the S.P.D. to restore ' Law and Order,' and filch from the workers the few important economic and social gains that had been won. We need only remember Ebert's law which practically abolished the eight-hour day. Ebert has done more for German Capital-ism that any pre-War Emperor. He saved its existence ! And then—they elected a Hindenburg !

" During these years, the Trade Unions have become vast mass organisations which were completely under the leadership of Reformist Social-Democratic bureaucracy. The Trade Unions were tools of the S.P.D., which by accept-ing the Government within a capitalist Republic, had at the same time accepted the responsibility for the continued existence of capitalism. Leaders of the bitterest enemies of the working-class ! Capitalism, as it were, gave permission to the S.P.D. to leave the servants' quarters and to enter

the drawing-rooms of the Government, where they sit
to-day, until the capitalists find the time is ripe to send
them back in order to use the sham opposition of the
S.P.D. leaders as best guarantee for carrying out the
dictatorship of Capital. The S.P.D. never can, nor will,
become a workers' party again, because its leaders, and
more than a third of its membership have become chained
to capitalist society through salaries and posts in the
State Administration. They are forced by the basis of their
existence to carry out the hunger and wage-cutting policy
of their bosses. It is obvious how important is the rôle
of the reformist Trade Unions in this connection. I have
here a shameful document of this co-operation between
S.P.D. and T.U. leadership against the workers."

He took a type-written letter from the table and held
it up for the workers to see.

"This letter has been sent by the A.D.G.B. (German
T.U.C.) to all branches that are Social-Democratic in
outlook. It runs : ' The Communist press, particularly the
Rote Fahne has recently been trying to make capital
out of the factory council elections, and they are proud of
their successes, especially in the big factories. The S.P.D.
press has approached us with the request to supply them,
through the help of the Unions with reliable material
(a few workers laughed ironically) which they can use
against the Communist press.' "

He replaced the letter on the table and looked
up.

"Shame," Kurt called out furiously.

"Damned swine, traitors."

"Just think—the swine ! That's what we pay our
contributions for."

"And they shout that the Communists want to split the
ranks."

It took some time before the speaker could make himself
heard again.

"Comrades, these to-day are the ' Free Trade Unions.' "

"We shouldn't pay another cent to these skunks,"
shouted the woman with the shawl.

" No, comrades, that certainly isn't right," the speaker replied.

" The only result of that would be that they would then be able to do as they like with our money without being in any way disturbed."

" Hear, hear ! "

" Do you simply want to desert your millions of working mates who have not yet clearly recognised the anti-working class role of the Trade Union leaders, and leave them at the mercy of these rogues ? No, just the opposite ! Just now before the 1st of May we must do all in our power to explain to our S.P.D. and unorganized fellow-workers, in the branch meetings, in the factories, on the streets, in trams and at the shops, what the real truth is and why it is that these same Berlin Trade Unions have the cheek to issue a manifesto for the 1st of May, in which they dare to write that ' Irresponsible parties call for demonstrations. No trade unionist will take part in these demonstrations.'—"

" They'll see. We'll show them ! "

The reserve which had been shown at the beginning of the meeting had completely disappeared. People had warmed up. Members of the audience were debating heatedly among themselves. Near the door a regular discussion group had formed, completely forgetting the speaker.—Hermann tapped his glass energetically.

" Comrades, we cannot carry on like this, we must have silence until the speaker has finished, afterwards you can hand in your names for discussion."

Some laughed, and then there was silence once more.

" Comrades, I shall now finish. Last year the T.U. leaders and the S.P.D. saw how the May Day demonstrations were completely dominated by the Revolutionary Trade Union Opposition, with their slogans and fighting spirit. From being a tame, orderly demonstration, it had become under our influence, and through the workers supporting us, a political revolutionary mass action. In the same way this year, a 1st of May demonstration in the streets of Berlin will show how small the influence of the reformists has become over the class-conscious workers.

It would become a day of struggle under the Red banners of the Communist Party. Such a mighty demonstration which would be directed in the first place against the starvation policy of the S.P.D. Coalition Government, and would be a blow to their prestige. Fearing this they have instructed their ' Comrade Police President ' to prohibit the May Day demonstrations.

" But, comrades," he raised his voice. " We Berlin workers did not allow ourselves to be driven off the streets by a Wilhelm, and we will not now let ourselves be driven off the streets by Zörgiebel."

" Bravo ! "

" Hear, hear ! "

" I repeat. We shall go on the streets on Wednesday. We shall go unarmed. And under the eyes of a police force armed to the teeth, paid for by our pennies and led by a Social-Democrat, we shall conquer the streets."

" Bravo ! Bravo ! "

The speaker's arm was outstretched as if in accusation over the heads of the workers.

" Comrades . . . when the S.P.D., through *Vorwärts*, lines up in the front of the reactionary press, with their countless lies and slanders about the alleged blood victims " desired " by the C.P.G., and paints the bloody shadow of a Noske or a Severing on the grey house fronts of the Berlin workers' quarters, then the day will come—when—as in Soviet Russia—the history of the Revolution will hold want over these myrmidons of Capitalism, stained with the red blood of workers, and pronounce judgment upon them."

" Bravo, bravo. Köslin street cell will be there all right ! "

The former tension had vanished. The room, thick with tobacco smoke, buzzed with intense debates. Hermann rose : " Comrades, you have heard the speaker's report. We now proceed to the discussion. Who wishes to speak ? "

He looked at the gathering. No one replied. There was a great deal to be said, but no one liked to begin. It was always like that. One encouraged the other. " Jupp, you begin." " Let Otto speak first." " Well, go ahead, Otto ! " Kurt rose and caught Hermann's eye.

" Comrade Zimmermann will speak."

Kurt began slowly and somewhat hesitatingly. He could speak more easily to his mates at work. " Comrades, perhaps this does not belong to the subject, but I think when we are considering the Trade Unions, we must also talk about the factories. You know that as far as we building workers are concerned, everything will stop on Wednesday, you know that. All of us in the job are going to the demonstration as one man. But how about the other trades in Berlin ? As far as I know 650 resolutions have been received from mass organisations and factories, including resolutions from workers' meetings at some of the largest factories, protesting against the ban on the demonstration. That is a good deal, but not enough by far. Our cell embraces a number of factories, in some of which there even exist Communist factory cells. What's happening there ? Why don't we hear anything about them ? We must use the remaining time till Wednesday to get something going there. Perhaps Hermann will tell us what should be done in that direction ? "

He sat down again. Hermann answered at once. In some of the factories, meetings had been organised which were due to take place before the end of the week. It was already quite definite that with few exceptions all work would cease within the area embraced by the Köslin local. In one case the Social Democratic factory council had refused and had told the workers that " in the interest of urgent orders in hand " work must not stop.

" A fine factory council ! "

" How much will the management pay them for that ? "

They would nevertheless try, by means of leaflets, to get the workers to stop work.

Everyone wanted to speak now. Even old Hübner, who had arrived late, took part. Hermann looked at the long speakers' list with concern.—After an hour he moved closure of the debate owing to the pressure of other important business.

They proceeded to the second point on the agenda : the preparatory work for the 1st of May ! Leaflets to be distributed in the mornings outside the factories, sticky backs were to be pasted up during the night. There was going to be a big meeting on Sunday night for which house-to-house canvassing had to be done, the May number of the " Wedding-Prolet," the local paper issued by the cell, had to be finished, printed and distributed. A great many tasks, all of which had to be done by the members after their day's work.

It was almost twelve o'clock before the meeting closed. Among those who had volunteered to stick posters was Kurt whose night finished at half-past five.

" I'll come over to your place in a few minutes, Hermann, I just want to let Anna know."

" There'll be a little row about this, won't there, Kurt ? " said Hermann laughing as he gathered his papers from the table.

" Why do you always tease me about Anna ? Perhaps she'll come too," answered Kurt. He was annoyed that they regarded Anne as a petty-bourgeois housewife, who did not understand anything about party work. He knew that one day she would herself reach a stage when she would join the party. They shouldn't always talk such rubbish ! But still, to-night she might perhaps make difficulties, he thought, as he went through the passage leading to the street.

Hermann stood and chatted to the delegate outside for a few moments.

Two more contrasted types could scarcely be imagined, than the broad worker Hermann and the pale little man who now stood with upturned collar, shivering in the cold. He told Hermann that he was working as a clerk at Lorenz's and had been elected on the works council in spring.

" Don't smoke so much," Hermann advised him good-naturedly, as the comrade offered him a cigarette and lit one for himself. He had seen in the flickering light of the match that the speaker's eyes were feverish.

" Well, what should one do about it, comrade ? " he

said with a tired smile, " I expect that many of you in this street can't boast of perfect health ! "

He looked into the dark, silent street in front of them.

" Good-night, comrade." He shook hands with Hermann, turned and disappeared in the darkness.

CHAPTER VI

THE BLUE SPIRAL

UNTIL Sunday night nothing in particular seemed to happen. The newspapers were read more carefully than usual, somebody or other would bring a reactionary paper into the " Red Nightingale " that would pass from hand to hand. No absurdities were too great to be printed in those days. The least that was said was that the communists intended " to have the revolution " on May the 1st. The *Vorwärts* was worst of all. There were several young Social Democrats among the workers who smashed the windows of the BADSTRASSE branch office of *Vorwärts* in broad daylight and under the eyes of the police.

On Saturday, someone hung the front page of the *Nachtausgabe** which carried as usual a blatantly provocative headline in the window of the " Nightingale." Above it was written " POISON—don't touch ! " Later, someone else wrote across the page : " Therefore only read the *Rote Fahne.*"

The discussion groups of women in front of the houses were perhaps somewhat more frequent and lasted longer, sometimes men also took part in these talks and told what they had seen and heard in the factories or in town.

The " town " was outside. The " town " began behind the Nettelbeckplatz. It was great Berlin with its motor cars, its traffic, huge stores, policemen, and some millions of people. The people from the alley rarely got so far. Going to work—if you still had work—was the only opportunity for most of them. Early in the morning, when it was still dark, they left, only to return late at night tired to the alley. There was a cinema round the corner. You

---

* Evening edition of *Vorwärts*.

could sit for an hour or so near the stove in Krückmaxe's shop. Finally there were the pubs. The Köslin quarter was a self-contained Ghetto of poverty. Although the Kösliner Strasse itself was fairly wide, it was always spoken of as the "alley." These twenty-three tenement blocks with their deep back yards had a population of thousands.

.   .   .   .   .   .

A few months before a certain Petrowski had opened an ice bar. A plain white-washed room on one side of which was the small counter with the ice containers. In front of the counter stood four little round tables and chairs painted red. The most important piece of furniture in the shop was the electrically driven ice machine which worked immediately behind the window. On the wooden fly wheel towards the street was a white cardboard disc of about three feet diameter with, painted on it in blue, a beautiful spiral. When the wheel turned round it looked as if the spiral were transformed into an ever-deepening, madly whirling funnel. The children who in the first weeks, pressed their noses flat against the window pane, became quite giddy, as they looked into the ever-quickening whirlpool.

At the back the room was partitioned off by a white-washed wooden wall. Behind this wall the owner Petrowski slept and lived. Perhaps it was a little unusual for such a small tradesman to have a telephone installed a few days after his arrival. It was never used by his customers. Whoever had to telephone, went to the "Red Nightingale."

Business in the shop was bad from the first. Petrowski placed bright paper flowers on his tables and took trouble to make his shop as nice and comfortable as possible. Yet the children who now and then came to buy a penny or a twopenny wafer preferred to eat it in the street. Only very rarely did someone sit down inside. Later, since the weather was too cold for the ice business, he tried his luck with cheap potato puffs. But in vain. There must have been something that prevented the people from feeling really at home in Petrowski's.

The whole thing was particularly curious when one considered the habits of the people of the alley. The bad overcrowded dwellings were no agreeable places to stay in during the daytime, especially for the young people who were often only lodgers. Moreover coal costs money which was badly needed for food. There were a number of small shops in the alley with a table and a few chairs near the stove. In Krückmaxe's cigarette shop — he was called that on account of his wooden leg—a number of young workers always forgathered. They smoked, talked and discussed. Above all it was nice and warm, a better place to stay in than a cold, narrow tenement. Again, the many pubs in this alley took the place of a sitting-room, or even of family life for many. And a pub's for drinking in— what else ? On pay day drunkards were sometimes to be seen in the alley. It was not by chance that the drunkards were nearly always those who misery was greatest.

But at Petrowski's—and this was certainly odd—the red chairs remained empty in the evenings. He was unpopular. Once he said he was a Hungarian emigrant who was not allowed to return to his country. He made it appear from his talk that some political matter he could not speak about, was the reason for his exile. Nothing more was to be got out of him. The black, pock-marked fellow was unsympathetic to the workers for some reason or other which no one could have given. His over-polite manner did not suit the alley and its simple inhabitants. The fact that Petrowski was a foreigner had nothing to do with it. The Polish worker Mitja at number one, was the friend of the whole alley, though he could scarcely speak a word of correct German. But there was a difference.

* * * * *

About six o'clock one evening, Anna was standing with her little son on the street outside the front door. It was terrible how dirty the alley looked even on Sunday. The side-streets of the workers' quarters were only cleaned once every few days. Foreigners and visitors never came here, so what did it matter ? The children were playing street-football with a leather case filled with rags.

A tall well-dressed man came along. He avoided the women chatting outside the doorway by making a small

circuit towards the roadway, and carefully scrutinised the
house-numbers. Then he slipped in the ice shop.

Anna had just noticed the man. She did not know him,
he did not belong to the alley. She had noticed that he
was looking closely at the numbers and ended in Petrowski's
shop. He looked like a tax collector she thought.

While Anna was gossiping with the other women, she
suddenly remembered that it could not have been a tax
collector after all. To-day was Sunday. She became interested. Here was something abnormal. The man did not
live here, what did he want in the shop, which even the
residents scarcely ever patronised ? Perhaps she would not
have taken any notice at all of the man if it had not been
for Petrowski, for whom Anna had an especial antipathy.
She looked undecidedly towards the ice shop. Dash—it's
worth it !

" Come, little 'un, you can have a wafer since it's
Sunday ! " Full of enthusiasm the little chap dragged his
mother towards the shop.

Inside the shop the first thing Anna noticed was that the
stranger was not to be seen. He was therefore not a
customer. He must be sitting with the iceman behind the
wooden wall. Apparently they had at once stopped talking,
for there was nothing to be heard. Petrowski appeared in
his soiled white jacket. When he saw Anna a friendly grin
appeared on his pock-marked face.

" Good afternoon, Mrs. Zimmermann ; glad to see you
in my shop ; times are bad, aren't they ! " He bent down
over the counter towards the little boy.

" Well, little man—what will you have ? "

Petrowski spoke German excellently, though his hard
gutturals betrayed him as a foreigner.

" A penny wafer," Anna said sharply, taking no notice
of his disagreeable friendliness. She was annoyed with
herself for having come. After all, what could she find
out ? Perhaps the man was a relative of the iceman on
a Sunday afternoon visit. Waste of money ! The boy might
even catch a cold in his inside from eating the wafer in
damp weather.

Petrowski handed the wafer to the boy with an exaggerated politeness.

Anna paid quickly and took Fritz into the street, sucking at his wafer, overjoyed at this unexpected gift. Looking back she saw the iceman behind the curtain of the door watching her.

"Idiotic business," murmured Anna, "the devil take it—there's something wrong with that fellow."

But what? He was not looking after her because she was a pretty woman. He wanted to see where she was going. Why had the man behind the screen not stirred while she was in the shop, why had they stopped speaking at once? She was puzzled. If only Kurt were here!

On the other side of the street she saw Paul Werner who also belonged to the street cell.

"Paul! wait a minute," she called to him and crossed the road. Paul lived in the same house as the ice fellow and might know how to deal with this matter.

"Good evening, Anna, Kurt come back?" he asked and shook hands in a friendly manner. He liked the tidy young woman.

"No, Paul, but I want to tell you something." She was reassured as soon as she saw that Paul had become serious and listened attentively. After she had finished he looked at her thoughtfully for a moment.

"Well, Anna, you can be sure that's a split! We've suspected for a long time that that fellow Petrowski didn't move into this street just by accident." He thought for a moment.

"Listen, Anna, you walk here for a while with your little boy, in case he is still watching. Afterwards, when he can't see you, go in the house from the other side."

Paul did not hesitate. Here was cause enough to investigate the matter. Damnation! That's all that's missing—a police spy in the middle of the alley equipped with telephone, and well-placed for street observation. Damned rogue! He worked himself into a fury before having the slightest proof. The otherwise kindly Paul Werner—he was the treasurer of the local—would have liked best to drag the two men into the streets, shouting : " Come and look all of you people—these here are police spies—bob-a-time Narks—who have been set for us, in this street . . . penny-traitors—who have been set for us, in this street . . . just look at their mugs . . . that's what the swine looks like, a member of our class too, but willing to sell his neighbours into prison for the measley sum of eightpence ! " Then he would like to bash their two spies' faces into pulp.

But keep calm, keep calm, Paul. Put your temper into cold storage and keep it dry. First think how to get at them.

He stood still for a moment and forced himself to think. There was no point in going into the shop. You wouldn't find out anything that way. By the yard there was only the lavatory window which was too small for anyone to climb through. Suddenly he remembered having heard the telephone clearly through a door which led to the back of the shop.

He went cautiously, close to the houses till he reached the doorway immediately next to the ice shop. He went in and closed the door behind him as a precaution.

There was only a faint glimmer of light in the dark passage. The door leading to the shop must be somewhere here on the right !

Paul felt his way along the wall slowly and noiselessly to the door. But even before he put his ear to the wooden door, he could hear a loud and excited conversation going on behind it.

" Well, I'm damned," he whispered in surprise. The iceman obviously did not realise that he could be overheard. Paul placed his ear by the thin cranny between door and wall. So long as no one passes through the passage just yet ! he thought.

" . . . No, it is quite impossible, there is no connection there. I have examined it carefully. You can really believe me ! "

Paul recognised the high-pitched, nervous speech of Petrowski. He almost stopped breathing with excitement. Now apparently the visitor was talking. Damn . . . the

wretch spoke too softly to be understood. That was the
cautious, low voice of an experienced 'tec who always
expected walls to have ears.

Petrowski again interrupted excitedly.

" But I tell you, it's impossible. The people must have
got through the houses in some other way—perhaps over
roofs—for there is no other way leading from number 19
to the Reinickendorferstrasse. I was there only the day
before yesterday and looked carefully. . . ."

The other by the tone of his voice seemed to ask a
question.

" Yes, that's not so difficult. The Panke is not very deep
around here, nor would it be very difficult to make an
emergency bridge with a few boards. Yes, you can reach
the Hochstrasse from there quite easily."

Paul could stand it no longer. He stepped back a pace
quietly. That's better, just catch your breath. He felt an
uncomfortable pressure in the neighbourhood of his
stomach. At moments of excitement he invariably was
attacked by a terrible internal cramp.

He tried to concentrate. Now we've got the cur ! There
could be no more doubt after hearing that conversation.
He must act at once. Someone must listen, while another
must let Hermann know immediately. Where on earth
can Anna be ? He still found it difficult to think in his
blind fury. The swine—sitting here in the middle of the
alley and spying on the houses. . . .

A furious attack of pain almost threw him to the ground.
It was as if someone was tearing his bowels out. He stood
in the passage bent forward in agony when the door opened
and Anna entered.

" Paul, what is the matter ? " she whispered in a fright.
He pressed his stomach with his fists. He pulled himself
together with all his will power. He must not give in now !
With difficulty he straightened himself and drew Anna a
few steps up the stairs on the opposite side.

" I took the boy home first," Anna explained.

" Good, good, Anna," he answered with a wave of his
hand. " Listen carefully—go to that door—very cautiously

—they mustn't notice anything. Listen carefully what they talk about. I'm going to look for Hermann."

His face was ash-grey with pain.

" Paul, let me run," begged Anna, who still did not understand what was the matter with him, though she saw that in this condition it was impossible for him to cross the street. Paul clutched her shoulder and pushed her down the stairs without a word. Once in the passage he pointed to the back door and then went quietly towards the gateway. He turned round once more. Anna was already hidden in the recess.

Once in the street he felt better. The pain was less agonising. It was the remains of a nervous trouble from the war, which could have been cured, given the necessary years of rest. Just when above all he needed calm nerves this terrible cramp always attacked him.

He first had to go to the " Red Nightingale " to hear where Hermann was. Perhaps somebody had seen him. He would use this opportunity to drink some soda water, the only thing effective against this pain. The attack usually ceased as soon as the soda water made him hiccup. Funny thing—but there it was.

He quickly ran down the street. On the way he enquired after Hermann. No one had seen him. The thought flashed through his mind for a moment of what would happen if he told the people in the street that two police spies were talking about the alley in the iceshop ! There would not be much left of the shop fittings. " No, no— Paul—that is wrong——" he muttered to himself, " first tell Hermann."

In the " Red Nightingale " Kurt Zimmermann replied at once to his question. " He is over there at home."

" Quickly—come with me, Kurt ! " He had forgotten all about his soda water now that he knew that everything was in good hands, he became calmer and the pains left him at once. On the way he told Kurt hastily what was the matter.

" Oh, boy ! If he knew the alley, he wouldn't have dared settle here."

"He'll soon get to know us," answered Paul with suppressed rage. Kurt took the news much more calmly. Of course the police would send splits and agents into the alley! After all, it was not the first time that they had been found out. The chief thing was to catch them and stop their dirty work.

In the iceshop a light was now burning. The shop was empty. Hermann lived two houses further along. Mrs. Süderupp opened the door for them.

"Good evening, comrades—Hermann is in his room."

From the door they passed through the one large room of the flat. Little Heidi, aged two, was sitting on the floor and playing some mysterious game with a large block of firewood. As Kurt stroked her hair in passing, she bent her head forward, annoyed at the interruption and went on with the game. Heidi rarely took any notice of the many grown-up people who were constantly coming and going. Daddy was next door. That was quite enough to make her happy.

Through the half-open door came the irregular clicking of a typewriter. Kurt pushed the door back.

In the corner of the little room, near the window, Hermann had built out of boxes a kind of bookcase. The centre shelf was lined with red paper and here stood a small bust of Lenin. This was, so to speak, the very modest "Lenin corner" of the Red Alley. Above the bust there were two rows of pamphlets, mostly party reports, speakers' notes and a number of Marxian scientific books. Jack London's "John Barleycorn" was the only novel there. The condition of the books showed that they were not put there as ornaments.

It was the typical bookshelf of a party leader who, as a worker, had no time to read any books but those absolutely necessary for his party work. Many a night the metal worker Hermann Süderupp had spent here in the light of the kitchen lamp forcing his weary brains to study the problems of "Surplus Value," "Capital Accumulation," "Post-War Imperialism," etc. "Without a revolutionary theory—no revolutionary party," said Lenin, a large photograph of whom hung on the wall, in an old frame. "Uncle N'in," as Heidi used to call him.

Next to the table there was a cupboard of papers of all kinds, newspapers, documents, leaflets. However often he cleared it up, it was always untidy. On Heidi's little table stood an old, second-hand typewriter on which Hermann was now typing with one finger, slowly, but correctly the text for the street cell paper.

The group leaders used to call this den " The Red Room." Quite out of place in these surroundings was Heidi's small teddy bear which was hanging from the ceiling on a string. They had won it in a sideshow at a fair, and because Heidi was then too small for the big bear, Hermann had hung him up here. Since Heidi is satisfied with whatever her father does, it had remained hanging here ever since.

.   .   .   .   .

Hermann saw at once from Paul's expression that something important had happened.

" What's the matter ? " he asked, pushing back the machine.

"There's a 'tec in Petrowski's shop. We overheard their conversation from the passage. The black scoundrel is a split."

Hermann stood up without saying anything, went to the window and looked for a few moments into the dusky yard. Someone was calling out of a window.—A spy in the alley. Of course that was to be expected, but still the news came somewhat suddenly.

" Anna is still standing at the door and listening," said Paul behind him. He turned round, his plan was made.

" Kurt, you send two young communists from over the road into the shop, they should sit down there, select little Fritz as one of them. He is very reliable. They're not to leave until the split has gone. But of course their behaviour must not be obvious. If someone sits in the shop they can't continue their conversation, and the fellow will go. Fritz is to look at him carefully. It would be good if one of you had a thorough look at the 'tec in the street in order that we know him in future. But careful, comrades, the swine must not realise that we have found them out. That's that. I shall go across to old Lederer in number 20, doesn't he work telephones at ' Mix and Genest ? ' "

" He's been there for eleven years."

" Don't you think the old man is reliable ? He's not a party member—but——"

Kurt looked at Hermann in surprise : " Whatever do you want that old chap for ? "

" Man, what do you think ? To deal with the 'phone, of course ! " Hermann replied. " Now quick. More this evening. First drive out the split. But, Paul, he's not to be touched. Don't make a mess of the thing ! "

" Of course not—Hermann, that's out of the question. Always keep cool ! "

Paul had regained complete control over himself. His pain had vanished. But he was glad they had the rogue.

When the three reached the street, Anna was already outside. She was on her way to Hermann. The police spy had just gone.

Hermann looked disappointed. " Now no one has seen him properly ! " He interrupted Anna who at once started to tell what she had heard of their conversation.

" Later, Anna—come upstairs with me. We meet in half an hour up at my place. . . . I must first go to number 20. Bring Otto along with you, Paul. Bye, bye ! "

He slowly crossed the street. It started to drizzle. The lights from the cinema signs were reflected in the wet pavements. Behind the rain-spattered window of the ice-shop the blue spiral was whirling.

.   .   .   .   .

Next morning a carefully hidden sideline leading to the second floor was connected to the thin telephone wire which ran down the house to the window of the iceshop. Old Lederer was a fine worker !

It was a good thing that Paul who lived two floors above Petrowski could only hear the conversations between the police and the iceman. Otherwise he might not have been able to resist the temptation of calling : " Hallo—the 145th street cell of the German Communist Party speaking. —God bless you, Mr. Police President ! "

POLICE-STATION NINETY-FIVE was some 500 yards from Köslinstrasse. Service on this beat was no soft job. Disciplinary transfers were more frequent than usual, generally because a constable had mismanaged some emergency and after that was afraid to go home alone. Some of them were sent here as a punishment ; and these were not men to make the street service of the older policemen any easier. Especially strong men known for their fighting exploits were drafted into the area whenever disturbances were expected.

On Monday morning while it was still dark, a lorry with straw sacks and mattresses was being unloaded at the police-station. An hour later two special detachments to be kept in readiness from 12 noon arrived. These young men were to accompany the local officers on their routine beats in order to get acquainted with the locality.

As lorries with the men arrived, the forty-two-year-old policeman Wüllner went to the window. He watched his young colleagues somewhat curiously as they jumped lightly from the lorries. From one car several large cases apparently of considerable weight were being carried into the house. Wüllner took small notice of these, for the first men were already arriving in the guard room upstairs. There were young, healthy faces bearing signs of a certain nervous tension similar to that Wüllner had often noticed during the war, when fresh reserves from home were moving into the front lines at night for the first time. Front-funk—it used to be called : a curious mixture of curiosity and fear, mingled with a certain degree of love of the sensational.

In the corridor rang the incisive voice of an officer. The men at once clicked their heels. The officer in command of the special reserves—Captain von Malzahn, a comparatively young man, in a well-tailored, dark uniform—disappeared into the room of the lieutenant in command.

The loud hilarity of the young police troops who were laughing and chatting as they made themselves at home in the station, had a hint of misgiving in it. Old Wüllner had been on street duty here in Wedding for almost ten years and had seen a thing or two. He did not feel particularly friendly towards the workers, especially those living in this area who caused nothing but annoyance and trouble. Either there was a row at the guardians' office, or at the Labour Exchange in the Schulstrasse, or in the public feeding kitchens, etc. The women were the worst. They thought nothing of spitting on the uniform of a police constable— and there had been worse things than that. But since his duty had taken him into the rooms and kitchens of the people, he had begun to look at many things with different eyes. He knew only too well that many of them had nothing to lose but their lives. Often it had seemed to him that death itself would be preferable to such an existence.

As he looked at the beardless faces of his new colleagues he remembered an event of four weeks ago. He was passing down the Reinickendorferstrasse on night patrol with two mates, when suddenly a small boy about six years old came running up. Although the cold cut to the bone even through the thick police overcoats, the child wore neither shoes nor stockings. He looked as if he had just jumped out of bed. Under an old jacket, much too wide, he wore nothing but a thin open shirt on his little body frozen white with cold. The boy shook and trembled with wild, heartrending sobs and among his disjointed words they could understand nothing but an ever-repeated cry of " Mammy, Mammy ! " He tried to drag the constable away. Wüllner had three children himself, his Hans was about the same age as this youngster.

" Probably the father is drunk and beating up the old woman," one of his mates said contemptuously.

" Better keep your finger out of the pie, Wüllner, what happens in a family is no business of yours. In the end

you'll only find yourself charged with disturbing the peace
of the house ! " But Wüllner took the little boy's hand, and
turned to his colleagues.

" You wait here—I'll just see."

One of them shrugged his shoulders : " Well, you're the
senior officer . . ."

The child led him up the stairs from a backyard.
Wüllner's torch lighted three flights of dirty steps ; and
last, a half-closed door. On a chair near a bed flickered
the dismal weakness of a kitchen lamp. He looked round.
It was the only bed in the low-ceilinged room. A clean
white table-cloth covered the chest. In the shadow of the
lamp-reflector, there was a white enamel washbasin, the
surface of which was covered with light red, frothy blood.

The light fell on the thin pallor of a woman's face. But
when the policeman placed the hand hanging from the
bed on the cover, he felt a small flutter of life in the cold
bloodless body. Too faint, however, to expect anything
from a doctor urgently summoned, but a certificate of
death, " *Section 2 : Cause of death : galloping consumption
and hemorrhage.*" No. The real cause was something
different, thought P.C. Wüllner. . . .

For over half an hour he had sat watching the white face
of the dying woman. The silence of the night was grim.

The woman's chin was pushed forward curiously. The
nose became thin and sharp. A thin light-red streak of
blood ran over the face out of the corner of the embittered
mouth—and then the faint movements of the sunken
chest stopped.

In a drawer he found a few wage envelopes from the firm
of Löwenthal & Co., costumiers :

Work delivered from 15th to 22nd March, 1929 :—

For eight finished dresses, size 38, at 2					
marks apiece	..	..	..	16 Mk.	
Advance ..	...	..	..	10 Mk.	

Balance   6 Mk.

Berlin, March 26th, 1929.

Underneath this there was a health insurance card:
" Mrs. Marta Fischer . . . widow ; born, 4th July, 1894,
occupation dressmaker." Horrified, he looked across to
the bed. This woman with the furrowed face of an old
woman—was only thirty-five. He had taken the sobbing
child with him to the police-station. Next morning he
was called for and taken to the municipal orphanage.

The half an hour spent in that room had made P. C.
Wüllner very thoughtful. What sort of a life must that
have been, which had left the dressmaker Marta Fischer
torn and broken, although only thirty-five years old !

.   .   .   .   .   .

The application to the northern district inspector for a
transfer to another area which police constable Wüllner
asked for on the same day, was refused.

" Don't you, a long-service man, feel ashamed of yourself,
flying from the enemy at this critical moment ? Take an
example from your younger colleagues ! Did you serve in
the war ? "

" Yes, sir."

" Well, then—you aren't afraid of these red hooligans,
eh, Wüllner ? "

" No, sir."

" If I had not received a good report from your superior,
I could almost believe that you felt sympathy for this
undisciplined mob !—Your identification number ? "

" 2304, sir." The district commander made a note in
his book.

" No sobstuff on Wednesday, you understand, Wüllner.
I don't want to hear any complaints about you !—
Dismiss ! "

Constable Wüllner paused for a moment in the empty
guard room. He was stunned. Of course he was a long-
service man. At the sound of this hated Prussian officer's
snarl, something snapped automatically in his brain.
Heels click, fingers stretch, chin up, chest out : Yes, sir. . . .
No, sir. . . . . Dismiss . . . hold your tongue . . . get out ! He
gnashed his teeth in fury. They that hammered well into
you " Flight from the enemy," the colonel had said to him.

So they were—enemies ?   The dressmaker Marta Fischer had also been an enemy ?

The door from the passage was suddenly wrenched open, the adjutant of the command entered. Wüllner came to his senses with a shock, saluted clumsily and left the room.

The colonel raved. The storm broke over the head of the surprised adjutant. " That's the fourth to-day, in my area, who wants to desert. Have these fellows suddenly gone mad, or what on earth is the matter ? And always it's my best men, the older ones, who have been on duty here for years."

" Pardon, sir," the lieutenant ventured to reply, " it appears as if the old service men don't get on with the emergency detachments. We have received reports from several areas that——"

The colonel flared up again : " Naturally we must ask these gentlemen for their permission to shoot up this red gang of Jews —No, my dear Boddin, the men have been corrupted by the blackguards, they have been stationed too long in this area. It's been too cosy here these last years—that's all ! "

" Certainly, sir," the adjutant hastened to reply, " all this silly talk of ' People's Police ' makes these fellows soft."

The colonel took a cigarette out of a silver box on the desk. With a short stiff bow, the adjutant offered a match to his superior.

" Thanks, Boddin." The colonel had calmed down a little.

" I think, you know, these damned newspapers are to blame. If you read what the whole press writes, with one voice from the *Deutsche Tageszeitung* to the *Vorwärts* about the—God forbid—revolutionary preparations of the Communists—fantastic nonsense, what ? This Jewish press of Ullstein and Mosse of course leads the way. Our men read the stuff, and naturally they become funky.—Well, it doesn't matter ! You shoot more quickly in self-defence. Even good racehorses are sometimes doped."

" Sir, don't forget our East Prussians, these country lads are certainly not ' proletarianised ' yet."

"Yes,—I believe we can rely on them," replied the colonel, "little von Malzahn is full of enthusiasm about his smart boys ! Now, Boddin, back to work. There's plenty to do. Give me the correspondence from the signature folder."

The adjutant stepped to the left of the colonel and handed him letter after letter.

. . . . . .

In police-station 95 there was confusion confounded. Everybody was at sixes and sevens. Where normally there were rarely more than 15 men at once, 150 had to find room. Till now there had been 6 plain clothes men attached to the station, including an officer of the political police. Now a large number of common informers were to be added, "bob-a-time Narks," as the workers called them, most of them being professional criminals, brothel keepers and so on, who lacked character even for these "trades." Having betrayed their own accomplices, they now depended entirely on the protection of the police.

From the talks Wüllner had with the young recruits he grew convinced that far more was planned than merely an enforcement of the ban on demonstration. These fellows talked of nothing but different methods of street fighting, shock patrol exercises, clearing the pavements. There was a hot dispute whether it was more advantageous to use hand grenades on stairs or rifles. One noticed that they had been trained for months in methods of civil warfare.

Most of them had not followed newspapers till they came to Berlin. The great majority were entirely apathetic politically, or rather did not know the meaning of politics. The name " worker " was for them identical with " enemy." Someone insisted that the May Day celebrations had been introduced by the communists after the 1918 revolution. Wüllner did not hear anyone contradict this nonsense.

He would like to talk about different things with these colleagues, but he was afraid. The harsh voice of the colonel still rang in his ears.

. . . .

Among the young policemen there was a temporary sergeant of about twenty-two whom Wüllner noticed especially, because he was always going to the window and looking down to the bridge.

" That is the Wiesenstrasse down there, isn't it, mate ? " he asked Wüllner who stood next to him.

" Yes—what you see behind the bridge—there by the Panke, that is the name of the little stream, flows, are the Köslinerstrasse tenements. Real slums," he added after a short pause.

The assistant sergeant stared absent-mindedly out of the window. Suddenly he turned round. His face had a strangely excited expression.

" Do you know . . . It's my first time in Berlin," he said in a low voice which trembled with hidden excitement. " It is a great honour for us East Prussians to have been called here in this dangerous hour. . . ."

He paused and looked in silence at his heavy peasant hands. Then he continued as if speaking to himself : " It is a queer feeling suddenly to have this . . . power, don't you think so ? Otherwise the town folks always laugh at us, especially those from Berlin—but they won't laugh I expect, once we start mowing them down ! In Insterburg I succeeded in hitting an egg on a bottle three times in succession with an army pistol at a range of fifty yards. By Jove, I am looking forward to the day after to-morrow ! "

Wüllner asked in astonishment : " But who told you that there'll be shooting on Wednesday ? "

The East Prussian looked surprised. " Ha, ha," he burst out laughing, " you're funny. The communists aren't all heavily armed for nothing, they won't attempt a revolution with pop guns ! "

Wüllner was getting quite nervous by now : " Who on earth has told this about the ' armed communists '——? "

" Well, Captain von Malzahn ! You know he told us a good deal more about this Red scum."

" Oh . . . ! "

Wüllner left the young policeman, one Jochen Schlopsnies

as he learned later, and went from the room without another word.

. . . . . .

When Wüllner returned in the evening from his first round, the inspector who valued the calm, reliable man, showed him a new police order from the District Commander :

Police District North, Dept. 1,
Bull, Nr. 2044/29,
26th *April,* 1929.

" Re offences against the demonstration ban it has been reported that the actions of individual policemen have not been sufficiently decisive. When stones were thrown by the mob, the police on duty made a baton charge, but neglected to arrest the ringleaders. The command is not satisfied with this, but is of the opinion that when a number of men have recourse to their batons, it should be possible to arrest, and bring in some of the demonstrators.

Signed : BASEDOW."

Wüllner was almost surprised to find that they did not ask even more. Slowly the situation began to dawn on him. He felt that what was planned was no less than a punitive expedition against the Köslinerstrasse, although those gentlemen were careful not to talk openly in these terms yet. He remembered quite clearly how the colonel, when informed at an inspection that on the first day of the ban on demonstrations, eighty red flags had been hung from the windows of the twenty-three houses in the Köliner-strasse, had gnashed his teeth and said : " Well, my lads, this scum will be cleared out on May 1st ! " That was clear enough.

Wüllner had three more months to complete his tenth year of service. He knew the Police Act which had been passed with the help of his Social Democratic Fraction by the Landtag in 1927 only too well. They would not be able to dismiss him on account of " insubordination " or " breach of discipline " as it was so glibly phrased. He had too long a period of service for that and a perfect character. But this shameful law contained a certain paragraph, number 11, which he knew by heart, so hotly had it been discussed at the time.

> " A police officer can be given notice of leave before completing ten years of service even if the conditions stipulated in paragraphs 9 and 10 are absent, if he does not possess the capabilities necessary for a proper discharge of his duties, especially the mental and physical freshness and the power of quick decision and energetic action, indispensable for the police service ; in certifying this condition the judgment of the superior officer is to be taken into consideration."

That was a fine bit of work ! Whoever refused to participate in this action would simply be declared devoid of the " necessary mental and physical freshness," and would then have to try and find a new job at the age of forty-two. They were caught all ways !

For a moment he wondered whether he should not ignore the official channel of complaint and go straight to the Police President personally. After all he was a Party comrade. He could not help laughing to himself. Not for nothing was it known to all the policemen that the reactionary colonel above all, was the intimate friend of the Police President. He might as well take off his coat for good, and hang it up on the wall. To make an attempt would only have the same result.

During the evening he discovered, when he was alone in the captain's room for a moment, that the big boxes that were placed there, contained steel helmets, hand grenades, two light, and one heavy machine-guns, and about 400 Carbines, Model 98.

CHAPTER VIII

BRICKLAYER TÖLLE GOES TO THE "ALEX"

CHANGING in the builder's hut on Tuesday morning, Kurt noticed that something was the matter with his fellow-workers. He was too tired to start talking to the others at once. He had scarcely found time to sleep. The street-cell paper, the " Wedding-Prolet " had had to be folded and bound. Anna had helped but still it was three o'clock when at last the stacks of papers were finished. The unemployed comrades would be distributing them at the factories and in the houses of Kölinstrasse that morning. They were ready for May Day here on the job too. It was understood that not a stone would be touched. The workers on the nearly finished skyscraper of the Karstadt Store in Neukölln had even decided to hoist a red flag on the tower to-morrow. It won't be easy for the others to get up there and to take it down. . . .

If only this last working day were finished ! From day to day the heavy work became harder and harder for him. He had rarely been able to sleep for more than three or four hours during the last week. Well, after the 1st of May there will be time enough for that. There was no help for it. In these days party work was more important than sleeping and eating. He tightened the leather belt over his old working trousers. It helps to keep the bones together.

. . . .

" . . . Even Jagow couldn't have done that better ! "
" You're wrong—he did say beforehand that there would be bloodshed ! "
" Just listen to this : ' . . . whoever in spite of this, attempts on the 1st of May to make the streets the play-
64

ground of his political passions . . . ' This lousy swine he calls the May Day celebration ' political passions ' ! "

Bricklayer Tölle flung the paper he had been reading to the ground furiously and wiped his broad hands on his trousers as if he had touched filth.

Kurt turned to him. What was this ? " Fritz, just give it to me, let's have a look " he said. Old Tölle he knew was a member of the S.P.D.

" Haven't you read it yet, Kurt ?—the Police President of Berlin to his people ? " said Tölle bitterly as he picked up the paper again. " I feel ashamed as hell to think that such a swine belongs to my party." He spat the juice of his tobacco through the open door of the hut.

Kurt took the *Vorwärts*, and while he read fury overcame him.

" . . . So according to the will of the Communists blood is to flow in the streets of Berlin on the 1st of May ! That must never be ! And therefore I again point out with the greatest emphasis that the existence of the ban on all open-air demonstrations in Berlin is due in no small degree to the complicity of the Communists. Whoever in defiance of this ban attempts to make the streets the playground of his political passions must fully understand that he runs grave risks for himself and his followers. I appeal urgently to the peace-loving population of Berlin, especially to women and children, not to participate in any attempted demonstration, not to stay on the streets unnecessarily, and to support the measures taken for the maintenance of law and order.—ZÖRGIEBEL."

The other workers looked at Kurt. He was organiser for the revolutionary trade union opposition and had gained a great deal of respect among his colleagues through his determined stand for the workers. Eight days ago he had been unanimously elected as delegate of the workers on the May Day Committee.

Kurt dropped the paper and looked up. " Boys ! that's a fine fellow. He wants to shoot us down and announces beforehand that only the Communists are to blame ! "

E

Outside the whistle of the foreman sounded. Some rose and went towards the door.

"Just wait a minute, chaps," called out Kurt. "The boss can wait a bit to-day. I think we've just got to settle something first. . . ."

The men stopped and looked at him.

"I suggest that we of our firm go and have a word with the Police President himself. Whether it will help or not, I don't know, but it is our duty as workers."

"Do you want to ask him to shoot with lollypops to-morrow, Kurt?"

"Go to the 'Alex' and bash his face in, that would be the thing to do."

Tölle rose slowly. It was plain that it was not easy for him to speak. "Mates,—Kurt is right. I propose that all workers are called together during the lunch interval in order to elect a delegation to go to the police presidium and submit a last protest there. I believe that he will see us and I believe that it may be of some use."

"That's what you think, Tölle!"

"Better go yourself to your comrade."

Tölle turned slowly to the young worker and replied gravely :

"Very well. I will go myself with the delegation . . . if you ask me to."

The foreman's whistle was heard a second time, sharply and impatiently.

"Calm down—calm down, old cock, the work won't run away."

"Good, colleagues, tell the others. At dinner time we all meet in the large hut." Kurt put on a working cap thick with cement dust. He knew only too well that this step would have no practical results, but politically speaking that was precisely the point of it. Old Tölle,—a decent chap—was to see for himself, what game was being played up there.

The sacks weighing a hundredweight and a quarter felt lighter than he had expected to-day. He said a few words wherever he met a mate. By lunch time all the workers on the job had read the article of the Police President in the *Vorwärts*.

During the lunch hour it was unanimously decided to send a delegation from the job to the Police President. Old Tölle, another worker unattached to any organisation, and Kurt, were elected. The foreman looked surprised when the three men asked for an hour's leave, but what could he do ?

. . . . . .

On the Alexanderplatz the steam hammers roared and thundered on the work of the new underground construction. 'Buses rattled over the bridging logs and underneath workers were crawling about the excavated gangways. Through the narrow passages between the hoardings swarmed the crowd. Local trains rushed over a railway bridge—propped with enormous beams—to pull up with screeching brakes in the station. Alexanderplatz—the madly-hammering pulse of work uninterrupted day and night, Alexanderplatz filled with smoke, dirt and noise, with harassed, rushing crowds.

On the south of the square is the massive, dirty red-brick block of the Berlin Police Presidium : brain and heart of Berlin's law and order. The nerve-centre with ramifications in every corner of this city with its four million inhabitants : card indexes, dossiers stacked in the cold grey offices, warrants, photographs and finger prints. Here were the offices of the Political Department IA, with the names of all prominent communists carefully indexed.

The red-brick building on the "Alex" swarmed with vermin and high officials. "Bug Castle" the Berlin population called it. Once the red Police President, Emil Eichorn, had ruled here, here Spartacus had fought, here countless revolutionary workers had been tortured and sentenced, and here to-day lived and ruled the man who wrote : " . . . So, blood is to flow in the streets of Berlin on the first of May ! "

. . . . . .

The policemen on duty at the entrance of the presidium looked suspiciously after the three workers who had walked

past and were disappearing in one of the long corridors.
Perhaps he ought not to have let pass without examination
those three suspicious-looking figures on the eve of May
the 1st.

Old Tölle did not feel at ease. The many doors with their
incomprehensible, maddening name plates made him
nervous. Gentlemen with sharp, rimless glasses ran through
the passages and looked strangely at the three workmen. A
police officer without cap and belt looked out of the door
of a room and called a clerk who turned at once and ran
back quickly.

" Pardon, sir . . . ! " the civilian clicked his worn-
down heels audibly.

Tölle had never before seen an officer without a helmet or
cap on. But here these gentlemen were at home, after all,
he himself would not run about with a hat on in his own
home. But somehow this shining bald head of the officer
disturbed him. . . .

They did not like to ask for the room of the Police
President and went straight on as if they knew the great
building as well as all the others did. The heavy boots of
the three building workers resounded on the stone floor.

They were lucky, for suddenly they found themselves in
front of a big grey door, to which a small white cardboard
notice printed with shining black letters, was affixed :

POLICE PRESIDENT

ENQUIRIES : ROOM 209.

Tölle looked for the paper in his pocket on which they
had carefully and neatly written the resolution of protest.
He was furious with himself. Damn it all, the Police
President was only a party comrade whom they had themselves raised to his present position. He would just go
into his room and say : " Good-day, comrade President,
we want to present this resolution to you. Look here,
comrade, I'm sure you will be interested to know what a
social democratic worker thinks of your proclamation. This
sort of thing is really impossible, comrade President . . . ! "

He had already forgotten that an hour ago he had spat in disgust at this "comrade."

"Room 209." They knocked and entered. Tölle was surprised that the President's ante-room was so cosy. He had imagined it to be far more severe and cold, something like the guardrooms at police-stations where one has to notify one's change of address. Behind a desk at the window sat a gentleman who looked at them in surprise.

"What is your business, gentlemen?"

Kurt remained purposely in the background. Tölle must go through this business himself. He pushed the bricklayer towards the front.

"We want to see the Police President," Tölle said, full of self-confidence. The gentleman at the desk looked at them politely.

"May I ask what it is you wish to speak to the President about?" Old Tölle became a little uneasy. The fellow was unpleasantly polite.

"We are a delegation from the men of the firm, Bergmann & Co., and have been instructed to deliver something to the President."

The clerk rose with a smile and said regretfully: "Well, gentlemen, I am extremely sorry, but the President is just having an important conference and must on no account be disturbed just now. But if you like to give me the document, I will certainly pass it on to him as soon as possible."

"No, that's impossible, sir . . ." Kurt intervened, "we have been instructed to speak only to the President himself."

Tölle searched in his coat pocket and placed an old soiled membership card of the S.P.D. on the table. "Here . . . take that in to him, when he sees that, he'll receive us all right," he said and looked patronisingly at the clerk, as if to say, "See that, my friend? You didn't know who you were talking to. But now hurry up. Your President's my comrade, see!"

The clerk took up the little book, read the name of its owner and pencilled a quick note on to the white edge of his blotter. Then he again smiled politely and returned the book with a slight bow. " I am really awfully sorry, gentlemen, but the best you can do is to leave your letter here."

Tölle looked round bewildered at his two colleagues.

" No, no, you give our kind regards to your chief and tell him we know what's on," Kurt said rudely. He had had more than enough of this. Of course he would not receive three simple proletarians in his holy of holies, to-day of all days when he had more important things to worry about !—He drew old Tölle out of the room and slammed the door furiously.

" The bloody crew !—Well, Tölle, this is your ' comrade ' President . . . he's now sitting together with his officers and planning everything for to-morrow's blood bath. Do you think that he'll sacrifice one minute of his precious time to see a mere social democratic worker ? "

When old Tölle was really in a rage he said nothing ; he merely spat tobacco juice. Unfortunately, as they came in he had taken his chewing tobacco out of his mouth and carefully stored it in a little tin.

The young non-unionist laughed. " Well, Tölle, have a good look round, perhaps this time to-morrow you'll be here again in the bug castle with your comrade—but behind the bars."

A few doors further on Kurt read another nameplate : Vice-President Dr. Weiss. Enquiries Room 203.

" Come on, mates, we'll just try this one," he said determinedly and knocked at the door. This time they did not stop to talk to the secretary in the ante-room, but seeing the door of the large adjoining room open they entered without further ado, and without taking the slightest notice of the desperate protests of the secretary.

" Gentlemen—I ask you—this is against all regulations ! "

" Blast your regulations," grimly thought Tölle to himself and pushed the little weakling out of the way with his broad shoulders. The heavy boots of the three sank noiselessly into the carpet.

An undersized man was standing at the window behind the long trailing curtains. Slowly he turned. A pair of frowning eyes behind pince-nez looked suspiciously at the three workmen who without any previous formalities were now standing in his room.

"Your business . . . ? "

Now Kurt took the matter in hand. He took a few paces towards the man.

"You're the Vice-President, Dr. Weiss, aren't you ? "

"That's right."

"We've come as a delegation from the building workers employed by the firm of Bergmann & Co., in order to protest against the ban on the May Day demonstration and against the Police President's threat of shooting ! "

The Vice-President took a thin black cigar speckled with green spots from his mouth, blew the smoke into the room and lazily waved his hand.

"I am very sorry, gentlemen, but that is not the business of my department. For that you must see the Police President himself."

Just what I have already told the delegation from "Josetti," "Manoli" and the workers of the "Berlin Building Society"—he thought to himself. Why do these fellows always come to me ? And his next thought was : the man in the ante-room is an idiot, he'll be dismissed at the next opportunity.

"The Police President does not receive Berlin workers, and since you are his deputy, we at least want to take back your reply to our colleagues."

The Vice-President looked in surprise at Kurt. Then he turned aside, carefully removed the snow-white ash from his cigar by touching the heavy bronze ashtray. "My reply ? I have already told you that this is entirely outside my sphere of competence."

Kurt grew angry. "But when all's said and done, you've surely had some say in this matter ! Do you agree with the ban, and the order ? or what is your own opinion about it ? "

The Vice-President looked for a few moments at the three workers.

His eyes passed from the grave looking face of old Tölle

down to his wrinkled and worn bricklayer's hands, which hung heavily down at his side.

"Yes, gentlemen," he replied at last in a curiously colourless voice. If I must tell you what I think—*I don't think at all!*" And after a short pause he added : "Talk to the chief about it, I can do nothing."

. . . . . .

Kurt would have loved to burst out laughing when they had left the room. "Did you hear that, Tölle ? He doesn't think at all! What is he here for ? He hasn't got to work with his hands, and he can't with his brains. Smokes poisonous black cigars and looks out of the window. 'Talk to the chief about it!' Talk to my uncle! Swine all of them."

The other young worker laughed at the sally. Tölle was silent. He was thinking that his comrades would hardly believe him, when at the next branch meeting he told them about this afternoon.

"The Vice-President without a head," laughed the young worker. "No he's got a head all right," answered Kurt, "but he's one of those respectable democrats, you know, who stops his ears with cotton wool when his chief gives orders to shoot. He can't stand the sight of blood— looks out of the window in the meantime and smokes. All one gang!"

Suddenly old Tölle had lost all fear of these uncanny corridors with their many locked doors, he hated the smooth shaven faces of the clerks who looked at him suspiciously, he hated the officers who rushed past him in their high-polished boots. Those were the boon companions of our " comrade " Police President, who clicked their heels before him and who to-morrow would shoot at him and his class comrades in the name of Zörgiebel and the old party.

"Swine . . . the swine. . . ." That was all he could say.

Outside on the Alexanderplatz the pneumatic drills hammered madly. High up on a roaring steam hammer working in the middle of the street by the Neue Königstrasse, there hung a small, blood-red flag.

PART II

BLOODY MAY DAY, 1929

" Events of this kind show clearly how armed insurrection against the despotic government does not merely develop as an idea in the programmes and heads of revolutionaries, but as the natural, the practical and the inevitable next step of the movement itself ; a result of the growing indignation, the growing experience and the growing courage of the masses."—LENIN.

CHAPTER I

FIRST ALARM

THE grey-blue dawn of the First of May rose over the empty street.

To-day is a holiday. People sleep two or three hours longer than usual. In vain shrieks the siren of the A.E.G. works in the Brunnenstrasse. The black stream of human beings entering the high iron gates every morning at six o'clock is missing to-day. The railway crossing at the Putlizstrasse Station generally swarming at this hour with hurrying workers, is deserted. The streets leading to Siemensstadt—empty and deserted. The shadows of the immense flywheels on the vast glass front of the " Turbine " works in the Huttenstrasse do not move to-day. The black claws of the cranes in the Nordhaven hang motionless in the cold morning air over the unrippled water.

The workmen's trains ran to the industrial districts according to schedule, but empty and pointlessly. In the first-class compartments there were only a few managers and engineers reading the articles printed like war-time reports, under sensational headings in heavy type.

" The inhabitants of Berlin have been warned ! According to the final proclamation of the Police President, ruthless measures will be taken against anyone making the slightest attempt to violate the ban on demonstrations . . . sufficient forces of special police have been drafted into the workers' quarters to ensure respect for the state authorities. . . . There is proof that the communists intend to turn the May Day celebrations into bloody insurrection."

One paper had printed two photographs in its top right-hand corner. To the left was that of Thälmann, the communist leader, and next to it that of the commander of the police, Heimannsberg. Underneath was printed the provocative question : " Which of these will rule Berlin to-day ? " In a few hours all morning papers were sold out.

The first noise in the alley came from the " Red Nightingale." At seven o'clock, Black Willi pulled up the heavy wooden blinds and stepped out into the street. He lifted his nose, as if to sniff the cold morning air. A few red flags hung out overnight, swayed noiselessly in the wind.

" Damn . . . what has become of the streamer ? "

He rubbed his eyes, but still he couldn't see it. During the night the workers had suspended a huge streamer across the street, showing a caricature of the Berlin Police President with the name " Dörrzwiebel " (rotten onion). This poster had obviously been removed by the police in the small hours when even the last and most active comrades had gone to get a few hours' sleep.

Willi slouched back into the pub and brought out a chair and two big red flags. He carefully fastened the flags at both sides of the entrance. This job he wanted to do himself. No one else was good enough for it. The iron sign over the window had already been covered last night with a red cloth. " Long live the 1st of May," was written on it in large white letters, and there was a painting of a clenched fist.

" The old shop looks all right to-day," he said approvingly looking at the effect, head on one side. Then he shuffled back in his old worn-out slippers from which he only parted when in bed, and started to clear up. The fresh air coming through the open door cleared the smell of stale tobacco out of the " Red Nightingale."

Half an hour later, Paul whistled across the courtyard for Kurt and Anna. The red curtain was still drawn across the bedroom window, they were still asleep.

" Pfffiiuu. Hi, Kurt ! "

The curtain was pushed aside a little, and Anna's fair, smoothly combed head looked out into the yard. She was furious. To-day, at least, they could have let Kurt sleep a little longer. He had only come home at four o'clock from pasting posters. What sort of a holiday was this, if one could not even sleep a little longer?

Kurt had woke up and saw her standing by the window.

" What's the time, Anna? " but he had already thrown off the bedclothes and got up.

" Anna, girl, we're sleeping in . . . quickly now." He stretched out for his clothes.

" But, Kurt, it isn't seven yet, lie down for another hour," she begged him. At this moment Paul whistled again.

" That's for us, just have a look. Has the newspaper arrived? It would be strange if it hadn't been confiscated to-day."

" Paul whistled," Anna said sharply.

" Shout across, I'll be there in a minute. Is there a clean shirt for me to-day, Anna? Oh,—here it is."

Anna shouted something across the yard. A window was closed on the other side. She went slowly into the kitchen and started preparing breakfast. But she did not seem to get on as well as usual. Her movements were almost mechanical and she had to pull herself together to get through the work properly. Kurt put on his best suit. He attacked his obstinate hair so long with a wet brush, that it lay flat to his head. A white shirt in the middle of the week filled him with a festive spirit. He was thinking that to-day the workers the whole world over were celebrating the 1st of May. If they could all come together—all those proletarians who were not moving a finger to-day for their exploiters! Boy, the Lustgarten would be much too small for them. And if all together they puffed out their cheeks the cathedral would splash into the Spree. . . .

He suddenly burst out laughing. Fancy, thinking such nonsense! He was quite mad this morning. And it would not be such a " peaceful " holiday to-day!—He pulled at his tie. These damned things—devil take them!

" Anna," he called, " just tie this damned knot for me." She was accustomed to help when his heavy builder's hands did not succeed with a job. But to-day she did not quite manage. He noticed that her normally quick, steady hands were trembling.

" But, Anna—what is the matter with you ? " He was really frightened. She looked quite upset.

" Oh, nothing, Kurt." She just managed to say this, then she collapsed. Her pride, her independence which she cherished so much, all was at an end.

" But, Anna ! " He carefully touched her shoulders with his hard hands. Such outbursts of emotion had not occurred before in their married life. If she had only made a row or would scold, all right ! That he would have understood, then he could have answered. There would have been a squabble—as there had been many a time before. Not but that this was the least appropriate moment for that sort of thing ! But, as it was, he was helpless. He could only wait for Anna to come to her senses, and become her old self again.

People moving on the steps and in the yard. On the third floor Jupp had his gramophone near the open window and put on the " Red Army March " played by a brass band. The whole house was whistling, singing, running about and making a noise. Someone shouted out of a window across the yard.

Kurt heard Paul whistling again. He wrote : " Ten o'clock outside the ' Red Nightingale ' " on a scrap of paper which he laid on the table next to Anna as she sat, all crumpled up, on the kitchen chair.

Only when she heard the door closing in the passage, did Anna begin to think again. She saw his old work-day jacket hanging from a nail at the door, and on the chair his green, washed-out pullover. She felt tired but relieved, as if a weight was off her mind. Sooner or later it had had to come. Now it was over. He had seen her at her smallest, her weakest. And—there it was. Another woman would have collapsed sooner.

She saw the note lying on the table. She smoothed out the piece of paper which bore his large, uneven letters and looked at the clock. There was still time.

.   .   .   .   .   .

As Paul with Kurt went out into the street, they were brought up sharp by the sight of a regular forest of shining red flags. There was scarcely a single window from which a red flag, however small, was not waving. From several windows large red streamers were hanging : " Down with the ban on the demonstration " and " Win the streets on the 1st of May." On one of them was painted a hammer and sickle and the legend : " Long live the Soviet-Union—Fight for Soviet Germany ! " On the corner of the Wiesenstrasse a red streamer hung across the street bearing in huge letters the words : " Red Front ! "

Men, women and children with red paper carnations in their buttonholes were standing outside the houses. Many children were carrying small paper flags which they had made themselves, showing a clenched fist, a Soviet Star, or a Sickle and Hammer. Even some of the small traders of the alley had decorated their shop windows with pictures of Lenin, Liebknecht, Rosa Luxemburg, or with a large red five-cornered star. Krückmaxe had decked out his whole cigarette shop festively for the occasion. The front page of the *Rote Fahne*—special May Day edition, was pasted up on the walls of several houses. The inhabitants were standing in front of it, reading the text and discussing it.

Between 9 and 10 o'clock, more and more workers were coming out into the surrounding streets, walking to and fro in loose groups on the pavements. Everywhere red carnations shone from the jackets of the men and the blouses of the women.

There was such a crowd outside the " Red Nightingale " that Paul could scarcely push his way through. A fine bloody idea, he swore to himself, to send Hermann to Brandenburg, to-day of all days, that out-of-the-way hole ! Hermann was the only man in the alley who was capable of keeping these masses firmly under control. Paul felt uncomfortable, he knew that he was not a leader by nature. He would do his duty wherever he was sent. But he noticed that the indignation of the people over the ban on the demonstration and the provocative proclamations of the

Police President was getting too strong. The slightest cause might lead to a dangerous explosion ! Outside the " Red Nightingale " he saw a considerable number of social democratic workers who had never before taken part in demonstrations organised by the Communist Party, but who to-day were obviously prepared to join the demonstration against the ban of their own party comrade.

At the door of the " Red Nightingale " a courier reported that a strong police force was cutting off all the streets leading to the Köslin quarter. In the Guardians' building in the Pankstrasse, a hundred yards away, a whole company of police was hidden. The Nettelbeckplatz had been turned into a police camp. In several houses of the Reinickendorfer-strasse flying squads had been stationed in the entrance halls. On the streets themselves only the usual patrols of the local police were to be seen, who at present were remaining neutral. From time to time the small mobile lorries of the police manned by six to ten officers dashed at full speed through the streets. It was their task merely to report on the situation.

Kurt, who was standing next to Paul when he received the report of the courier, did not fail to notice the undecidedness of comrade Werner. He knew Paul as a reliable old party comrade, nevertheless he had not considered Hermann's choice correct when the night before he had appointed Paul as deputy leader of the street cell for the 1st of May. Paul was the oldest party member in the cell and had lived for over twenty years in the alley. He had only remained silent about Hermann's suggestion because he did not like to offend an old comrade. But he knew already that it had been a mistake. The situation was likely to become very serious, and in a case like this all personal considerations had to be dropped. He decided not to leave Paul for one moment during the day and to help him as best he could.

In the " Red Nightingale " you could have walked on the heads. The rooms were overcrowded with workers with caps and jackets decorated with red carnations or badges. Ten minutes ago somebody had discovered a

" split " in one of the rooms ; he was soon thrown out into the street, after a sound beating up. One could sympathise with the workers outside for repeating the dose a second time. Only in the Reinickendorfer-strasse was he liberated, by a police patrol.

Whenever a split was discovered, the police were not long in coming to his rescue. Kurt saw that it was a great mistake to have made the " Red Nightingale " of all places, which was known to the police as a party centre, the meeting place ! Now, when the situation was still undeveloped it would have been very easy for the police to surround the house, arrest all those inside and thus to separate the political and organisational leadership from the masses.

In the small hall at the rear, Kurt and Paul met the other comrades of the street cell. Old Father Hübner had also kept his word. He sat at the table in his black and shiny Sunday suit with a red carnation in his buttonhole ready for the signal to start. Kurt could see that much was passing through the old man's mind. For the first time in forty years he was to participate in a May Day demonstration which had been banned by a social democratic Police President . . .

" Thomas ! " Paul shouted through the passage. His voice was completely drowned in the noise. He pushed his way through the workers and approached an undersized comrade, wedged in a group in heated discussion. It was Thomas, the organiser of the marchers.

" Thomas, how are things with your people ? You are certain that none of them has anything hidden on him. We march unarmed."

Paul did not say this, because he was afraid. It was the strict instruction of the Party, and Hermann had especially warned him only the night before, to insist that on no account should anyone carry arms in the demonstration.

" Well, you know, Paul," Thomas answered as he tightened his belt, " I can't look into everybody's pockets. I have warned them about it not once, but ten times, at

F

least, and I don't think that there's one who has anything on him."

" Keep your men firmly in hand, Thomas—we'll have a good deal to face outside." The faces of the two workers were grave, a tremendous responsibility rested on their shoulders.

Paul looked at his watch. " Ten o'clock, Thomas, give orders to form the ranks. Time to start."

There was a movement in the masses outside when the door of the " Red Nightingale " opened and the workers streamed out. A woman shouted something out of a window. Everybody pushed his way to the pub.

A penetrating whistle cut the air twice in quick succession. They knew this signal. That was Thomas.

" Close the ranks. Forward march ! "

At once disorder ceased. The sound of the whistle gripped the masses like a steady, controlling hand, called them together, formed them into marching columns, put each in his place, and turned the feeling of nervous apprehension into that of ordered security. A three-cornered red flag which appeared in the front between the third and fourth rank was greeted with loud cheers.

The commanding voice of Thomas suddenly pulled all together. For a moment there was almost uncanny silence. Like the resounding blow of a hammer the short command rang out clearly and sharply over the heads of the ranks standing eight abreast.

" Attention. Quick march ! "

The first step was the signal for an outbreak of wild enthusiasm. The windows were thrown open when the rhythm of the march beat against the walls of the houses. A resounding young voice shouted : " Down——with the ——demonstration ban ! "

There were some who shuddered as the whole street shouted in unison : " Down . . . down . . . down. . . ." A thunderous roar of protest !

The black mass of the workers taking up the full width of the street surged forward. At the head, the three-cornered flag glowed like a dangerous red-hot spark in the sea of grey, pale faces. Two or three began, then the whole street was singing the song of the " prisoners of want "— " The International . . ."

In the Reinickendorfer-strasse the blinds rattled down before the windows of the large shops. Iron bars clattered as they were drawn in haste across the entrances. The bloody May Day of 1929 had begun.

. . . . . .

Those looking out of the windows noticed it first. They suddenly started to shout excitedly, and to wave their arms. The marchers could only see their open mouths and terror-stricken faces, for their voices were drowned in the song. At the corner of the Reinickendorfer-strasse appeared helmets and silver uniform buttons. At the same time blue uniforms were seen behind the demonstration, coming out of the Guardians' building in the Pankstrasse. The shriek of a woman's voice from a window cut the air : " P-o-l-i-c-e ! "

Heads flew round. The mass wavered, the shriek of terror threatened to create a panic. Women and children pushed and knocked into one another. A girl was trodden underfoot. Her thin, plaintive voice was drowned in the angry shout of the workers who saw now that they had fallen into a dangerous trap.

It was a cunning, brutal attack. The police had blocked the short street on both sides and had wedged in the masses, now incapable of moving. As in a hunt, the surprised human beings were now driven towards the centre. Every-one saw at once that the police did not intend just to break up the demonstration, for in that case they could have left one side of the street open, but men, women and children were to be beaten down like defenceless cattle.

Whistling, screaming, booing filled the street, and then the terrible blows of the batons began to crack on the heads. Those in front pushed backwards, those in the rear tried to run forward driven by the batons of the police. A terrible panic spread.

Kurt jumped on to the steps of a house and placed his hollow hands to his mouth to make himself heard. It was useless.

In mad flight, the people rushed the house doors and tore them open. The screams of women and children increased the chaos. Few in the terrible crush were able to get into the houses. Batons broke heads relentlessly and so great was the press that those who collapsed could not even fall to the ground.

Kurt saw the distorted and furious faces of three policemen immediately in front of him. " Get down—you swine ! " shouted one of them at him and pulled him from the stairs. At the same moment three police batons crashed on the back of his head. Anyone else would probably have been done for.

Kurt howled with rage—turned . . . and before he knew what he was doing, his broad, hard fist crashed within an inch of the helmet's edge, against the forehead of a policeman, who collapsed with his mouth wide open.

Another, besides the policemen who now rushed up with drawn revolvers, had noticed this scene. It was Thomas, who was trying in vain to stop the panic, and had to be content to hold up the onslaught of the police from both sides as long as possible, in order to get the women and children safely into the houses. Before the other policemen arrived he had dragged Kurt into a passage and slammed the door behind him.

The dark passage and the stairs were crowded with people. " Quickly," Thomas shouted, as he pressed his broad back with all his might against the door, " All of you, get into the tenements."

He had to kick Kurt before he could get him to hide somewhere.

The raging young policemen outside could not move the door. They rushed back into the street, cursing.

In the middle of the almost deserted street a woman was pressing to her breast a wailing infant. In vain she had at first tried to push her way into one of the houses ; with difficulty she had escaped from a perilous crush, and now the doors were firmly closed against the police. In the street only policemen with drawn revolvers and swinging batons were to be seen.

Outside the " Red Nightingale " was drawn up the transport lorry on which they were lifting the policeman Kurt knocked out. He had not yet regained consciousness.

The woman with the child had now almost reached the end of the street, when suddenly a twenty-year-old policeman ran up to her. Her face lost all its colour, but she wound her arms more firmly about the child and went on. It was apparently this firm self-control that maddened the young policeman. With a jump he blocked her way, raised his arm . . . and struck her across the silent white face.

" Back—you red sow," he shouted and pushed the woman who had unconsciously raised her arm in self-defence.

From the windows horrified spectators were watching. " You hound—you'd kill your own mother——" an old woman shrieked.

" Bloodhound ! "

" Blasted swine, you ! "

And suddenly a big stone crashed into his grinning face. Then revolvers cracked. Peng . . . peng . . . peng. . . !

The first shots ricocheted against the houses. " Close the windows ! " The young policeman with a stream of blood running across his pale, terror-stricken face, ran up and down in the middle of the street. He aimed at every movement he could see behind the windows, and fired.

The street was now occupied only by the police. There was not a civilian in sight. In some houses the police had chased the inhabitants upstairs and across yards, right into the rooms. Out of one of the houses they dragged a young worker covered in blood and threw him on the transport. Earlier on, they had arrested two carpenters, and they were now both sitting there in the lorry in their traditional dress with their top hats bashed in.

Out of the Pankstrasse pealed the long-drawn whistle of the commander, twice in quick succession. Slowly and almost against their will the police withdrew from the street.

.   .   .   .

A few minutes later the street was again filled with excited crowds. The brutality of the police and the mean cunning of this attack had aroused the indignation of the whole neighbourhood. Angry groups formed themselves on the street.

" That was only the beginning," a woman called out.

" You wait—this evening the *Vorwärts* will say that the police acted ' in self-defence.' "

" Thank your ' comrade ' Police President for that ! " an old working woman shouted into the face of a man who was standing by.

" Don't you worry," he answered quietly with a helpless movement of the hand, " I believe—I won't be a member of that party by this evening."

From another group one could hear Paul's loud voice : " Comrades, we ourselves are to blame, we should never have started a demonstration in such a short street which can so easily be cut off."

A few workers were going inconspicuously from group to group : " Re-form the ranks—at the corner of the Reinickendorfer-strasse ! " The new command was passed quickly from mouth to mouth. The workers were gathering on all sides, their faces more serious and determined than ever.

Again the penetrating sound of the whistle gave the signal to form the ranks. The workers ran quickly into the roadway and formed themselves in rows of eight : " Quick march ! "

From the Nettelbeckplatz glittered the silver ensigns on police helmets.

" Down . . . with the . . . May Day . . . ban ! "

" Long live the Communist Party ! "

" Down with the social-fascist starvation government ! "

This time the shining uniforms did not startle the workers. Calmly they marched down the street towards the Nettel-beckplatz to the strains of the " International." For a moment Kurt thought he noticed Anna's fair head between the workers' caps in front of him

As they passed the Co-operative Store, a frightened face

disappeared behind the iron-bars of the window. It was the manager—a Social Democrat. The workers laughed and shouted across the street : " Celebrating the 1st of May behind iron bars, eh ? "

" Like monkeys in the zoo ! "

Again five or six rows in front of Kurt the fair smooth head appeared. Then it was hidden again by the next regular wave of surging heads.

" Hallo ! Morning, comrade ! "

A narrow hand was stretched towards him across a couple of shoulders. Kurt looked up. Wasn't that the pale young speaker, who had spoken in the " Red Nightingale " ?

" Red Front ! " He drew him to his side.

" Come on, it will start again in a minute ! "

He was glad to see how the young, certainly not very strong comrade was marching so calmly next to him. He doesn't only talk, thought Kurt, satisfied.

The demonstration was approaching the Nettelbeckplatz. Kurt stretched for a moment to look above the heads in front of him. The police were standing four deep across the street awaiting the demonstrators.

The workers continued marching forward without a moment's hesitation.

A high-pitched voice screamed in front : " CLEAR THE STREET . . . ! "

The workers marched on. Left . . . left . . . left. . . . " Down with the police dictatorship ! "

That was Thomas, thought Kurt, and shouted with the others : " Down . . . down . . . down ! "

On the right pavement some began to run backwards. Someone shouted :

" Stand . . . firm . . . comrades ! "

The centre of the demonstration pushed further and further to the front. The first broad rows were formed by Thomas' men. He himself was marching next to Paul at the head.

Again the high, sharp voice whipped through the air— some command—and the batons crashed down on the first rows. There were piercing noises of booing, whistling and shrieking ! Against a house on the left a gentleman with a battered hat was leaning and gesticulating wildly in ridiculous protest. Apparently he had just come out of the cigar store at the corner. Two policemen tore him away from the wall. He collapsed under a hail of blows. A policeman was kicking his hat like a football over the square.

The police wavered. In spite of their mad rush at everything in their way, they could not break up the demonstration. On the contrary they were forced to retreat step by step before the ever-increasing pressure of the masses. The workers protected themselves as best they could, but they did not budge an inch. If they were pushed back in one place, they pressed forward in another.

The police only succeeded in breaking up the demonstration after fresh reserves had been called, though they still could not clear the street. The whistle called them back again. A few curt orders and they jumped into the waiting lorries and drove away. Possibly the situation was even more dangerous elsewhere.

A few minutes later a young worker had jumped on a sand box in the centre of the Nettelbeckplatz and spoke to the masses who filled the square.

. . . . . .

Kurt was looking for Paul. At last he had found him.

" We must return to the alley at once, Paul,—we must see what is happening there." They knew that the police attacks would be concentrated there. They hurried back along the Reinickendorfer-strasse.

After a few hundred paces they noticed that the workers in front of them were running towards the alley. They followed them, running as quickly as they could. At the corner of the Wiesenstrasse they met a new demonstration coming from the Uferstrasse.

" Paul, that is Otto—that one with the flag in front ! " Kurt called out and ran towards the marchers.

He had not yet reached them, when he heard the nailed boots of the policemen running behind him.

Only reach the demonstration ! he thought pantingly.

He was too heavily built to run quickly. The young police-men could do better.

" I'll get you yet, you bloody swine," someone shouted close behind him. He heard the loud breathing of the policeman. The next moment the baton fell on his head. But the policeman ran past him towards the demonstrators who had now reached the corner of the Köslinerstrasse.

The policeman who was about ten yards in front of his colleagues rushed straight at the flag bearer. Kurt saw him raise the baton against Otto.

What followed happened so quickly that no one could tell how it had come about. The young policeman was suddenly lying on the street without his helmet on and rolled over several times. Just then other policemen ran up. Shortly before they had hit a man to the ground from behind, a few paces in front of Kurt, and had belaboured him with kicks and blows.

" Get up, you dirty skunk——" roared a policeman. The man could only whine and kept pointing to his feet. Kurt noticed that he had a wooden leg.

" I'll teach you to run," the policeman shouted and rained blows on to the helpless man. Only when he saw the other policeman rolling on the ground, did he leave prostrate the man who was a disabled ex-service man and rushed at the flag bearer.

Kurt lifted the man, who was groaning with pain and carried him into a house. " Here is my address. You can give my name as a witness. It won't help much, those swine don't stop at perjury. But you can try." He scribbled his name and address on a piece of paper which he pushed into the man's pocket.

At the corner of the Köslinerstrasse raged the fight for the flag. Otto shouted so that it could be heard even in the backyards. He struck out with one fist, with the other he clung to the miserable, torn little flag. Kurt saw that blood was running from his scalp, but Otto did not let go.

There was a sound of singing from the other side of the Köslinerstrasse. A new demonstration had come from the Pankstrasse and was marching down the Weddingstrasse.

Kurt tore a small red cloth which he had taken with him as signal-flag from his pocket, and waved it to the comrades marching on the other side, in order to call them to the rescue. " Come this way ! " he shouted with all his might, through the alley.

The marchers at the other end of the street stopped. The workers looked up in doubt, they did not know what the man with the flag wanted of them.

Suddenly Kurt heard a terror-stricken shriek behind him : " Kurt ! "

He turned quickly. At the corner of the Wiesenstrasse stood Anna, and pointed in horror behind him. Several policemen were running straight towards him with raised revolvers. He knew that in their mad rage they would shoot him down without hesitation. He ducked and reached the nearest door—number six.

" Stay where you are . . . you dog ! " shouted the police-men behind him and took aim with their revolvers.

Peng . . . peng . . . peng . . . Right and left the mortar flew from the wall. Kurt ran through the passage. The glass door to the yard was smashed in a thousand pieces as he slammed it.

" Kurt, they are following ! " someone shouted from a window into the yard. He heard the nailed boots in the passage. The yard was as smooth as a plate. Just as he was in the middle, they shot again.

Peng . . . peng . . . A cold rush of air passed his brow. The plaster flew in white powder from the wall near the entrance to the next house.

" Back from the windows."

At the very moment the policeman fired at the window Kurt sprang back to the stairs. The quick warning from above had probably saved his life. On the first landing he was drawn into a flat and hidden. He could hear the policemen rush past the closed door and up the stairs. In an attic they tore the washing from the hands of a terror-stricken washerwoman and even out of the steaming boilers, to look for him there.

.   .   .   .

Anna had managed to hide herself in a passage when she heard the shots from the house on the other side which was sheltering Kurt.

" Do you want to be shot dead, too ? " a worker shouted at her as he held her back from the open door.

" Let me go, Max," she said, a curiously low, hoarse voice. " Do you hear, Max—let me go ! " She tried in vain to bend aside the fingers round her arm. New shots rang out. Anna looked at the worker for a moment, then she beat his face twice in succession with her free hand. He fell back to the wall, and tearing open the door she rushed out. At the corner the flag bearer and another young worker were being arrested and thrown on the police lorry. The flag was in a thousand shreds.

Four police vans came rushing down the Wiesenstrasse from the Ufer-station. Their sides flew down while they were still running, the corner was cleared with pistols and batons.

Anna saw how the policemen were coming out of number 6, again—without Kurt ! A paralysing thought struck her. Where was he ? Why had they not taken him with them like the flag bearer just now ? With an effort which almost overpowered her, she forced an image out of her mind. She had seen him lying in the yard, face turned downwards. . . .

People rushing past her carried her with them.

" Down . . . with the . . . starvation government ! "

Policemen ran after them with drawn batons. Someone fell to the ground. After a terrific baton blow the raised head fell with a hollow sound back on to the pavement. There he remained lying.

" Three cheers for the Communist Party ! "

They shouted, the whole alley shouted, and Anna with the others. " Hurray . . . hurray . . . hurray ! " When the police had driven them from one side, they shouted on the other. They shouted from the windows over the policemen's heads. A red flag was shot down from the second floor ; a woman tore it up from the pavement.

Peng . . . peng . . . peng.

The round bullet holes on the grey house fronts were like white pock marks.

. . . . .

The loud echo of the shots alarmed the workers of the surrounding district. More and more reinforcements came into the alley. Those coming from town reported that the police were attacking the workers everywhere with the utmost brutality. On the Hackesche Market they had fired into the demonstration of the tobacco workers. Three workers dropped,—one was dead. In Kliems halls on the Hasenheide they had fired into the meeting of the plumbers. A woman told how a demonstration had been broken up with bloodhounds only ten minutes away, in the Badstrasse. It was said that armoured cars had been used in Neukölln. Trams had been upset by the workers. People who came from the indoor meetings of the trade unions in which not a word of protest had been heard told how they had been met at the very entrances of the halls by policemen who batoned them. Anyone wearing a red carnation was a target for the police. In the Kleine Tiergarten in Moabit they arrested forty carpenters in one swoop and rushed them off in cars to the police presidium, although they had participated in a meeting sanctioned by the police.

Police lorry after police lorry rolled into the Köslin quarter. Wherever they jumped off and batoned the workers, the masses closed behind them again as soon as they went on. On the Nettelbeckplatz a worker who was supposed to have shouted something was arrested. As the police car drove off with him, he clenched his fist surrounded as he was by the police and shouted to the workers on the street : " Red Front." He was not silenced till, as the car rushed away, they knocked him senseless.

Near Wedding Station the police turned on the hoses and attempted to disperse the workers with water amidst a pandemonium of whistling, booing and mocking laughter. The police vans which dashed through the streets, were greeted with piercing boos by the excited masses. Ever new demonstrations formed themselves which were dispersed after marching a few hundred yards, only to be reformed afresh. The workers had learned to evade the rushing police and to expose themselves as little as possible.

The following happened about noon :—

Until the police had cleared the entrance to the Reinicken-dorfer-strasse on the Nettelbeckplatz, the street was full of policemen with drawn revolvers. In the centre of the empty road a trembling young girl who had just come out of a shop was attempting to get out of the danger zone.

She hoped to get out of the danger zone first safely under the protection of the police cordon. The workers watched. She was a civilian who had blundered by accident into the beleaguered area. A policeman suddenly gave chase.

Terrified, she turned round and started to run with helpless trembling little steps. The policeman reached her in a few strides. He shouted at her and struck her on the head from behind. She ran across the street under a hail of blows, towards the pavement. After about twenty paces she was at the end of her strength, swayed, and fell with her back against a house wall. Her head fell exhausted to one side. Again the policeman shouted at her, but she could run no further, through fright and pain. He raised his baton once more and struck the girl with all his strength in the face—a face dead white and numb with terror. The back of her head cracked against the wall, her hands gripped the air, and she collapsed.

At the corner, the road was up and from this direction a hail of sharp stones flew through the air. The helmet of a commanding officer lay in the mud. A stone crashed into the middle of the provocative silver ensign.

The officer whipped out his pistol : Peng . . . peng . . . peng . . . The workers retreated into the alley before the onslaught of the police. But this time they locked the doors behind them. Again the revolvers echoed between the walls. In the deserted street, red flags were hanging like flames on the grey houses. From corners and invisible hiding places hundreds of eyes were looking down on the raging policemen who rushed about firing into the houses. Although not a single civilian was to be seen in the street, they continuously shouted : " Clear the streets . . . on peril of your lives . . . ! "

A window in the third floor of number 19 opened and a worker looked calmly down on the police. He smiled in a friendly manner and called out :

" Hallo !—Friend ! "

Two policemen were standing outside the house. They at once raised their revolvers and took aim at the man in the open window. For the fraction of a second the light spot of his forehead was in the line of sight ; a finger pulled the trigger : Peng !

The worker's hand dropped, the head fell forward on the window sill, and the body capsized slowly into the room. The window was empty. . . .

The policeman stared into the gap which had so suddenly swallowed up the face. He looked round in terror, called out something to the policeman next to him, and both ran rapidly down the street.

A few minutes later, the police had withdrawn. The alley was again empty and filled with an uncanny silence.

.   .   .   .   .   .

The door of number 6 was hastily thrown open. Kurt ran over the street and disappeared in number 19.

He ran upstairs. The door stood open. Some neighbours had arrived already. Under the window-sill lay in a pool of blood the fifty-two-year-old plumber Max Gemeinhardt, member of the Social Democratic Party of Germany and of the Reichsbanner. Deathly silence filled the room. A thin streak of blood marked the white window-sill, and in it dabbled a fly.

Someone drew Kurt quietly out of the room, it was the woman who lived next door. Outside in the passage she whispered : " *Kurt—did you see who fired that shot ?* "

For the first time to-day Kurt was trembling. He leant against the wall in the dark passage. It seemed as if his brain was still refusing to take in the horrible fact. At last he said hoarsely :

" I saw him. I recognised him . . . Mother Hübner—
that was *Murder !* "

.   .   .   .   .   .

Ten minutes later, Sergeant Haberstroh of the Ufer
Station and another young colleague received an immediate
order transferring them to another district. From that
moment Sergeant Haberstroh never again entered his
father's house, number 3, Köslinerstrasse, which till then
had been his own home.

Sergeant Haberstroh and his father were also members
of the S.P.D.

CHAPTER II

THE WOMAN WHO LAUGHED

THE news of the shooting of the plumber spread like wildfire through Wedding. It spread to the shops, to the stations, and to the trains in which frightened people carried the news to other parts of the town. It penetrated to the back houses, up the stairs, into the dwellings of workers, the dwellings of the bourgeoisie.

"Do you know . . . have you heard about it . . . ? The police shot a man in the red alley—straight in the face and he is dead. . . ."

They came running out of the houses. Here and there groups of men and women surrounded a worker who was telling how it happened. In the workers' pubs it was no longer so calm as it had been in the morning. There was scarcely one man who had not seen for himself how the police had to-day, on the 1st of May, become the enemy of the people. A dangerous nervous tension marked the faces of the people moving in large crowds through the streets surrounding the Nettelbeckplatz. For over an hour after the fatal shot no policeman was to be seen in the vicinity of the alley.

More and more people came into the Köslinerstrasse to look at the houses on which the white round bullet-marks of the police were to be seen against the dark walls.

The window in the third floor was closed. Hundreds of people stood in the street below and looked up. Immediately above the closed window a red flag was flying. As it swayed slowly in the wind and was lifted to one side, someone pointed a finger towards it. In the red cloth could clearly be seen four round holes against the sky.

Outside the butcher's shop at the corner a crowd had gathered. An unknown voice was speaking to the workers.

" Bravo ! " someone shouted.

" He's quite right ! "

Kurt coming out of the " Red Nightingale " with Anna,— after the police had retreated he had found her in the street—glanced at the crowd. He had been looking in vain for Paul and Thomas to discuss the situation. He was fully convinced that the position in the alley was getting more and more dangerous every moment. At any moment the police would return and no one could possibly tell what would happen. It was essential that they should keep the leadership of the excited crowds firmly in their hands.

" Someone is speaking over there," Anna said to him. Those outside the butcher's shop were laughing and applauding. Then Kurt heard the loud sharp voice begin again. His attention was now aroused.

" Who is that ? "

He crossed the street to the crowd and pushed his way to the front. On the steps of the shop, the blinds of which were drawn, was a man in a black leather jacket. His unhealthy, bloated face was red with excitement. From time to time his oily voice broke into a falsetto screech. " Funny bloke," thought Kurt.

" That won't be the only one," the fellow in the leather coat was shouting. " And are we to fight with bare fists against revolvers and machine-guns ? "

" Quite right," a woman shouted.

" Only revolvers are of any use against revolvers."

" Bravo ! "

For the first time this dangerous, provocative word had fallen and it found ready soil. An excited discussion followed. Everyone shouted at once. Yes—he is right. Shoot down these murderers of the workers ! Just as they shoot us. It is only self-defence. Are we to wait till more of us are lying dead on the ground ? Kurt elbowed his way slowly forward.

" Comrades . . . " the fat one shouted and pointed his

finger over their heads, " over there in the Ufer Station there are plenty of arms and ammunition . . . Come on—let's get the stuff ! "

In the uproar of applause that followed, Kurt pushed aside those in front of him and gripped the fat man by the arm.

" Leave him alone. He's quite right," a woman shouted. The fat man had turned pale and was trying to get away.

" Stop.   Stand still ! Who are you ? Where do you come from ? "

The man tried in vain to free himself from Kurt's firm grip.

" Let me go ! " he groaned, " Can't a bloke say what he thinks, don't you think so, comrades ? I'm a worker meself," he suddenly began to speak in the Berlin dialect like a proletarian.

" What—a worker ? " Kurt shouted so that all could hear him, " just you show your hands ! "

A few children were running across the street and shouted : " There they've caught one." Kurt tore the hands from behind the back of the other, held them tightly round the wrists and saw fat, rosy fingers with the mani-cured nails. A worker who was standing near by called out : " With those you can only work on your old woman in bed ! " There was a burst of laughter.

" Damned provocateur !" roared Kurt, " coming here to incite the workers. You swine ! " In the same moment the fat one crashed against the blinds of the shop, his cap slipped comically on one side.

" Look out. The swine wants to shoot ! " The split had put his hand into his hip pocket. With a howl of pain his right arm dropped. Kurt's second blow had caught his shoulder. Now the other workers started. They realised that they had nearly fallen into the trap of a provocateur.

" Into the passage with him," someone shouted.

" Kill the swine."

" He must not get on the street again."

A few steps further on a house door slammed. The people who had gathered in front of the house were at

once dispersed by a young worker : " Comrades—go away !
There's more than one split in the street. The police will
soon be back again in any case."

Out of the passage came the sound of muffled blows and
the screams of the split. Shortly after, a young worker
in the " Red Nightingale " who had somehow aroused
suspicion, barely managed to save himself in the last
moment from a similar fate. One among the Red Front men
present happened to know him since he worked in the
same factory. Strange faces aroused suspicion now. Too
many plain-clothes men mixed with the workers in the
neighbourhood of the alley, and not all the bob-a-time
Narks were as clumsy as the fat one outside the butcher's
shop.

. . . . . .

About three o'clock the loud singing of a demonstration
coming from the Wiesenstrasse into the Köslinerstrasse was
heard ; it was led by a young communist. Everybody ran
down the alley to meet the demonstration. Again the
windows flew open, again they shouted " Red Front ! "
and waved downwards with their flags. In military
formation with closed ranks the marchers passed through
the alley gathering more and more men and women as they
went along.

Anna ran by the side of the demonstrators. She was
thinking how curiously the demonstration changed at once
the expression on the faces of the people in the alley. The
nervous tension had vanished. All at once they felt
themselves filled with a sense of a new conscious, confident
power, through the steady rhythm of marching shoulder
to shoulder.

For the first time in her life Anna felt, as she marched
through the alley with these thousands, a strong wave of
elation rising from her heart to her burning eyes. It was
a deep inner feeling of happiness that almost dazzled her.
This, she thought, is the cause of the sudden light in the
ashen faces. And she was happy that she was now going
through the same experience. . . .

She had not noticed that the demonstration had reached

the Reinickendorfer-strasse and was now returning to the Wiesenstrasse. Only when the singing suddenly stopped and the people around her started to boo, to whistle and to shout : " Down with the murderers of workers ! " did she see the police helmets glittering closely in front.

She was seized by fear, but not for herself—for the others, for all, for the comrades who were now picking up stones. Someone shouted : " Stand where you are, comrades ! "

She was pushed to the front with the others. The calm light had vanished from the ashen faces. A piercing woman's voice shrieked from a window : " B-L-O-O-D-H-O-U-N-D-S ! "

Like a torn gust of wind the shrill voice echoed above the heads of the masses. Out of the Reinickendorfer-strasse, behind them, the long-drawn signal of a police van was heard. Somewhere, far away, she heard a thin, cutting voice : " Fire."

The young man in front of her turned round. The red spot in his buttonhole danced before her eyes. It became larger and larger. A red circle in mad rotation. . . .

Peng . . . peng . . . peng . . . The quick firing of police pistols cracked straight into the masses.

" O—o—oo ! " the worker before her clasped his stomach and collapsed with a painful groan. A few yards further along, the pale hysterical face of a policeman appeared.

A stone tore the smooth, beardless skin, his helmet flew off. Funny—how light his hair was above his bleeding face. After that Anna could remember nothing.

The police stormed over her, onward. Bullets and batons cleared the street. Behind them dark forms of bodies in cramped positions, faces on the ground, were lying in the roadway. From under the stomach of the shot young man a thin streak of blood trickled into the grey dust. A few paces further on an unshaven face the colour of ashes stared with wide eyes into the blue sky. Foaming red bubbles burst from the open mouth. The blunted bullet getting him in the back had torn his lungs. One man tried to crawl to the side of the street with a shot knee. A child ran aimlessly and screaming across the street with a drooping hand, apparently broken. Someone was calling for the ambulance.

Four or five young workers carried the wounded carefully into a house. The colourless head of the man with the gurgling mouth hung backward. Three dark puddles remained on the empty street.

In the alley the police were running past the quickly locked-up doorways. Shots cracked between the high walls like the furious barking of mad dogs. The enemy was invisible, the street empty. Behind the dark windowpanes lay the dangerous, hated enemy. Under the helmets the faces were terror-stricken. Before them—behind them—above them—crouched the enemy. The reds were waiting—hundreds—thousands—the whole alley is full of them—the town. . . .

Peng . . . peng . . . Trembling fingers automatically pulled triggers. The explosion makes a man feel strong and secure. As long as the shooting continues the grey faces of the enemy remain invisible. Only the flags remain—the accursed, hated red rags !

" Down with those rags ! " an officer shouted. Volleys rang out on the flags. A split flagpole snapped. Like a shot man it hung against the wall.

" Away with the flags from the windows." Glass jingled, mortar spurted through the air. Suddenly—a howl of rage from a hundred voices. A huge flag had fallen on the street from the fourth floor. The young policeman who picked it up and began to tear it, grasped the back of his head with a scream. He had been hit by a sharp-cornered stone.

The inhabitants drew the tattered red flags into the windows, lest they fell into the hands of those blue devils below. But over the entrance to number 3 a small red flag was still shining from the first floor.

" Down with the rag ! "

" Take the flag down ! . . ."

Four, five of them shouted one after another. The windowpane crashed on the pavement in front of the house. But the red spot did not disappear from the grey wall. A soft wind raised the small four-cornered cloth and made it swell as if it were mocking at the powerless fountains of lead.

And suddenly something unexpected happened. Something that was more terrifying and dangerous for the police than anything else. A woman laughed! Somewhere as if in the thin air, a woman laughed. A short resounding burst of laughter, the expression of a provocative feeling of strength that was certain of victory. Like a bird the bright sound hung over the heads of the frightened policemen, then it died away and was gone.

All in the street had heard it, its echo resounded from the house fronts, climbed up the walls in the back yards, rang in the rooms and cellars, and all at once the colourless faces of the proletarians became alive and strong again. . . . Go on shooting . . . shoot, shoot, murder, kill. . . . Whom do you think you are killing? Can you shoot our *slums* . . . our *hunger* . . . our *diseases* . . . our *unemployment*? You murderers of workers! Long live, Long live what you can never kill with revolvers or cannon: LONG LIVE THE VICTORY OF THE WORLD REVOLUTION!

And now the faces of the young policemen paled. The unknown, invisible woman who had laughed aroused a cowardly, paralysing fear. They started shooting again, madly, furiously, against the walls, into the dark windows, through bolted doors.

In number 3 where the flag was still waving above the door a flattened leaden bullet went through the house door and hit the leather belt of the worker, Albert Heider, tearing a hole as a big as a fist in his stomach. There he lay behind the large dark door, his legs pulled up and from the body entrails were hanging like pinkish coloured jelly.

CHAPTER III

PAUL AND LENIN

AN hour later, the police were drawn out of the alley, because of a large demonstration in the Reinicken-dorfer-strasse. They were kept systematically busy in the more distant streets by the workers, and were thus kept away from the alley for a time.

The workers realised that the alley which had no side streets and only limited possibilities of escape through backyards, was a dangerous mousetrap for them. They were driven there, to find themselves exposed without protection to the revolvers of the police who had cut off the street at both ends. The Wiesenstrasse lay across the Köslinerstrasse like the stroke of the letter T, and made a blind alley. Moreover the houses were no longer a sufficient means of protection, since the police had begun to storm them and to follow the workers into the tenements. On the one side of the alley one could at best reach the Wedding —or Reinickendorfer-strasse by way of the backyards, and these streets were easily kept in check by the police. On the other side the backyards were cut off by the Panke. And even if the fugitives waded through the water they would only reach Panke—or Wiesenstrasse.

It was easy to see that the surrounding of the whole block of houses was no difficult task for the police, and sooner or later it would surely come to that. What then ?

In numerous rooms in the alley, traces of bullets were to be seen on walls and furniture. Several children had already been hurt by flying pieces of mortar. Immediately above the bed in which a twelve-year-old child was lying, four bullets had crashed through the wall and covered the child with fallen plaster. It was sheer luck that more people had not been wounded or killed.

To remove the children now from the alley would mean carrying them through the firing zone. On the stairs crying, desperate mothers were standing cursing " the blue devils " below.

" Are you men ? " they shouted to the workers.

" You're white-livered, cowardly curs, who let the women and children be shot ! Throw stones like little boys and run away ! "

" You've muck in your bones instead of blood, you sots ! Because these lousy swine hold cannon in their hands, you rather dung your trousers than take the things away from them—you ' communists ' ! "

" You don't understand——" the men could only reply. " We can't simply start a revolution on our own to-day ! "

" No—but you can make grand speeches all right."

Then the men went out into the street again and thought to themselves : Right they are, those women,—but *cowards* ? No, we aren't cowards. The Red Alley isn't cowardly, not that—but—what shall we do ? What on earth shall we do ? Damned cossacks ! They were asking it on the stairs, on the yards, in the street, in the pubs— in the " Red Nightingale."

The narrow passage of the " Red Nightingale " was thronged with excited faces. The crowd was drawn towards the light of the electric lamp over the corner table. Thomas was carrying his bandaged hand in a leather strap hanging from his neck. Next to him sat Paul, whose cap was lying somewhere on the Nettelbeckplatz.

" Comrades—" Kurt was saying calmly, "—in a few hours it will be dark. If the police remain in the alley by then, you know what will happen. We won't have two dead in our houses to-morrow, but twenty perhaps."

He paused for a moment and looked into the faces of the workers around him as if to read their thoughts, then he continued : " It seems to me, comrades, that the police must not be allowed to enter the alley again."

" You're right, Kurt."

" Comrades, that is sheer madness," Paul shouted, and

jumped up excitedly, " Do you want to start a civil war on your own ? I protest——"

Thomas pressed him back in his chair : " Just be quiet for a moment, Paul, we'll see what Kurt has to say."

Kurt looked at Paul with stern brows. He was thinking of the workers standing around the table who knew that Paul was the deputy leader of the Communist street-cell for to-day.

" Comrades," I said, " the police must not be allowed to enter the alley any more. We—not the police—must block the street. Particularly we must prevent cars from entering ! "

" Yes, that's the chief thing, those damned police tanks."

" There's building material at the corner. We must build a barricade across the street at once, like this." He pressed the large forefinger of his broad builder's hand on the wooden surface of the table. " This is the alley." He drew a line with his finger, " and this the Wedding—' and this the Pankstrasse."

The finger drew an irregular triangle. The workers gazed intently at the scratched, spotty table and followed the invisible lines of the plan.

" And here," he tapped on the wood with his broad nail, " we build a barricade—from here to here : and a second one from the corner there, across to here, and the third straight across the entrance to the alley. Then the whole corner is blocked up and they can't enter either from there or there ! "

Attentive eyes followed the broad finger-tip on its travels across the table.

Kurt looked up. His face was no longer so calm as before. He knew that his plan implied a decisive sharpening of the struggle, but there was no other way out if they wanted to protect the populace from further police terror— a terror which, as experience had taught them, would grow fiercer and fiercer towards night. Before the last attack some people had already started to place wooden poles across the street. Kurt knew the people of the alley too well—they would not look on calmly for very much longer while one after the other was shot down, without resistance. He had seen and heard enough just now on the stairs and in the yards.

Thomas stood up and banged the fist of his sound arm on the table. " Settled, Kurt—get on, boys, to work—we haven't a second to lose ! "

The workers pushed their way out of the pub, taking with them everyone who was standing about. " Quickly—get out all of you ! There's work to do outside ! "

Everyone shouted and ran about excitedly. The atmosphere of helplessness and despair gave way at once to a strong, determined feeling of power.

.　　.　　.　　.　　.　　.

Kurt and Paul remained alone at the table. The room was quite empty ; from the front-room he heard Black Willi polishing his glasses. Kurt would have preferred to go out at once with the others, but he did not want to let Paul sit there passive like that. He had to have a quick word with him. The matter was too important.

Paul slowly lifted his head and looked at Kurt. His face was quite changed. Then he began to speak with a low voice trembling with excitement : " Kurt—do you know what you have done ? For what follows *now* I refuse to take any responsibility. You know that I have been in the movement for twenty years. I am not a coward, do you hear ? " His voice was raised threateningly. " I am not a coward, but I won't take part in *that !* "

His face was colourless. Kurt looked at him in surprise. Why did Paul speak in such a strange manner ? He bent down slightly towards him and placed a hand on his shoulder.

" Paul, what is the matter with you ? The whole alley knows that you are no coward. But—just listen to me— you have not yet clearly realised what has happened outside to-day, on the 1st of May. We in this alley aren't the only ones, everywhere in town the police have been acting like this. What do you think, Paul, what is happening in Neukölln just now ! And why are they doing it ? And why have they prohibited demonstrations on the 1st of May,

of all days ? And why do the S.P.D. leaders with their
Social Democratic police president, let the police loose on
the workers with the order to shoot ? "

Kurt was now shouting at Paul. He caught him by the
shoulders with both fists. " Why on earth, Paul ?
Because we Communists are to-day the only leaders of
the revolutionary workers. Don't you understand, Paul ;
to-day they want to smash us, so that the masses run away
from us, leaving us completely isolated, like a general
who suddenly finds himself without an army ! They are
beating down women and children and all the time they
mean the Communist Party. The Reichswehr, the police,
all are brought into action against the Communists, who
are ' inciting ' and mobilising the masses against the
starvation government of the social fascists."

Suddenly he was struck by an idea ; he searched his
pockets excitedly and finally took a few printed pages from
the many papers and cuttings that filled them. He
smoothed a crumpled newspaper page on the table. Across
the page ran the headline : *Lenin and the May-day celebration !* It was to-day's May-day number of the *Rote
Fahne.*

He had marked a passage printed in display type in the
top left-hand corner with a thick pencil mark when he
read the article early in the morning. He now pointed his
broad finger to this passage. " Here ! here it is, Paul ! "
He read aloud, slowly : " Events of this kind show clearly
how armed insurrection against a despotic government does
not merely develop as an idea in the heads and programmes
of revolutionaries, but as the . . ." he made a short pause and
continued with emphasis: ". . . the natural, the practical
and the inevitable next step of the movement itself, as a
result of the growing indignation, the growing experience,
the growing courage of the masses. *The courage of the
masses,*" he repeated with force, emphasizing every word
by tapping his finger on the table.

" And who wrote that, Paul ? Comrade Lenin wrote that
for the workers of Moscow when he commented on a
political mass strike in 1902. Do you understand now,

Paul ? The revolution does not come, as if Stalin said,
' when I press a button to-day there is armed insurrection in
Germany,' but it must grow gradually, with every action,
with every economic struggle, with every political mass
strike—and that's what the 1st of May is. It's no holiday,
Paul, out there on the streets ! Why don't the workers sit
still any longer, now they are being shot down and
batoned ? " He banged his flat hand on the paper in front
of him. " The growing indignation of the masses ! And
if we of the Party don't see this, then we are lagging behind
and they will lose confidence in us. But we are the leaders
and must always be at their head." And as if he wanted
to summarise all he had said, he continued : " *Self-
defence —Paul—is not armed insurrection !*—but only in
this way will we grow in strength, until one day we shall
be able to give up the defensive and go over to the attack ! "

Kurt was silent and looked self-consciously out of the
window after his long speech. Presently he turned round.
Paul was still looking at the paper in front of him. In
large, bold type five letters headed the article LENIN !
He saw the masses on the streets, the batoning, shooting
police, the red flags shot down, the worker Heider lying in
the dark passage on the floor with his torn open belly. . . .
He saw stones in the hands of the proletarians.

Paul was a functionary of the old social democratic
school, raised in the long-past revolutionary days of Social-
Democracy. His thoughts and feelings moved within the
limits of the old accustomed methods of agitation and
struggle. He felt himself that they were out of date to-day,
that what he saw outside required completely new tactics.
The capitalist system of to-day with its intensified exploitation was putting the youth through a harder training in
the class struggle than those who had gone before. Perhaps
Kurt was right, after all ! He did not grasp it all quite as
quickly. But, it was true. There on the page it was printed
in plain language, language everyone could understand.
And then—Lenin had said it !

He rose and went with Kurt into the street in silence. . . .

CHAPTER IV

MAJOR B. HOISTS THE WHITE FLAG

WITH a hollow crash the advertisement board fell across the street. The big, heavy iron sewer pipes which lay in preparation for repair work in the Pankstrasse were rolled up. Beams and boards fell noisily to the ground.

" Look out, comrades ! "

Crash,—the heavy builder's waggon lay on its side at the entrance of the alley like a huge, lazy animal, its wheels stretched helplessly in the air. With a splintering of glass, street lamps fell into the street. Hundreds of hard hands helped. Pickaxes tore up the hard asphalt. Sand flew from the shovels and was piled up in irregular heaps which were stamped into shape by the women. From a distant street shots were heard. The sound only hastened the work.

Slowly the barricades grew up in the shape of an irregular triangle outside the " Red Nightingale." They blocked the Weddingstrasse, the alley and the entrance from the Pankstrasse.

For days an old, torn mattress had been lying in a backyard. Two women now carried it along and threw it on to the barricades. Out of the houses came the iron dust bins— useful obstacles ! The workers scrambled between the heaps of sand and the beams. Women helped to pile up stones torn from the pavements.

Everyone laughed when they saw two young workers run down the street with a large gate which they had lifted from its hinges.

" Jupp, won't you bring along the beds as well ? " a young woman called out after them.

" You bet your life. If we take your bed, the bugs would carry away the whole barricade."

" Don't say that. My bed is first class. It's stood many a bump, though not from the police ! "

They laughed and shouted over their work. Packing cases, old baskets, sticks, boards, everything they could lay hands on was rushed to the spot. An old woman went with bent back along the street and gathered up stones in her apron. The window of her little flat looked out on the street immediately in front of the barricade.

The shooting came nearer. Thomas sent off a group of young workers with instructions to keep the police away from the alley as long as possible. He was no longer as calm as at first. He had had to take a gun from the pockets of more than one of the men. There was no time now to explain to them that the barricades were designed merely to keep out the police lorries. Against the present weapons of the police, barricades were no longer a special means of protection, particularly in a regular street fight. Much less were they a base for an offensive.

" Hallo . . . Thomas ? "

" Where is Thomas ? "

He turned round. The workers standing on the barricade were calling for him. He hastened across to them. A courier with a bicycle was standing on the other side. When he saw Thomas he dropped the cycle and ran towards him. His young face was covered with sweat.

" Thomas . . ." he said in a low voice when he was standing in front of him . . . " two cars with a machine-gun mounted on the first are on the way from Wedding Station ! "

Thomas scarcely waited for him to finish. He turned round to the workers : " Comrades—back into the houses at once. Lock the doors. The special detachment into the back room of the ' Red Nightingale.' No one is to shoot. Watch the street ! The street to remain empty ! " A few young workers ran along the alley : " All into the houses. Lock the doors ! "

The loud penetrating signal of the police cars was now

heard from the Nettelbeckplatz. The bright faces turn grey. The danger had suddenly returned like the dark shadow of a great revolver pointing towards the alley. . .

A young woman with smooth blonde hair tore up two little children who were playing in a puddle before the fountain.

Anna had fetched all the children living in number 6 and had taken them to the relatively safe room of a worker who lived facing the Panke in the second yard. She was now running about the street gathering all the other children she could find.

"Come here at once, you young rogue!" she shouted after Hermann's twelve-year-old boy, who had been in the thick of it all day long.

"No, Mrs. Zimmermann, the back-end is no place for me," the boy shouted back laughingly and slapped his pocket, which was crammed full of stones, with his dirty little fist. He ran into the "Red Nightingale" with the men.

The doors had not all been closed yet when the first police car took the corner of the Pankstrasse at full speed. The brakes screeched as they tore the heavy lorry back. Scarcely a yard from the car there lay, a silent menace,— the barricade! The alley beyond was deserted. Only from the windows the red flags were again flying, they moved gently, almost playfully in the wind.

There was deathly silence. The motor continued to hum and sing in the same indifferent and monotonous way. From their hiding places and corners the workers saw in front of them the faces of the police, which looked like white spots on the cars. The other lorry came along and stopped just behind the first. Waiting, puzzled, undecided, terrified——"

Through the glass-pane in front of the driver's seat the eyes of Major Beil wandered across the barricade into the silent, deserted street. Minutes passed before his brain grasped the fact that straight in front of him the street was blocked by a large, wide barricade. And what—what was *behind* the barricade?

He felt his hand in the leather glove grow moist with

perspiration. This expectant silence was unbearable. Why did that gang in the alley not whistle and howl as usual ?

" Damned nuisance—a fine intelligence service ! " He jumped out of the car.

" Wüllner."

" Sir ? "

" I shall negotiate. At the sound of the first shot or when I blow the whistle, you storm the barricade ! "

" Very good, sir ! "

" Look out, Wüllner, where I go . . . "

He turned and went towards the barricade. The leather strap of his helmet stood out, a dark line on his colourless face. In his hand he waved a white handkerchief !

Hundreds of invisible eyes were fixed on this white spot which suddenly appeared outside the barricades. A trap ? Capitulation ?

The door next to the " Red Nightingale " was opened and Thomas came out.

For a moment they stood opposite one another in silence. The grey jacket of the proletarian with its crushed red paper carnation, and the blue, immaculate uniform of the officer with its silver epaulettes. One on one and the other on the other side of the barricade. They looked at each other across a black iron pipe.

" Are you the leader ? " The sharp military voice of the major was not as provocative as usual. At present he was not standing there as victor.

" What do you want ? " The major took a step towards the barricade.

" Stop ! Stay where you are ! " Thomas called out sharply. He knew that the officer wanted to look at the strength of the barricade. The major stopped at once. " If you clear the barricade, I shall give orders for my men to withdraw for that period."

" Only to storm the street afterwards, isn't that so, Major ? " Thomas replied mockingly. " The barricade will remain until the last policeman has disappeared from the whole of Wedding and until you give us your guarantee that the workers can demonstrate without interference ! "

" Bravo ! "—The major turned round startled—a woman's voice from a window. He again turned to Thomas and said nervously :

" I guarantee that you can clear this whole thing away without interference."

" You know our terms, Major ! " The door next to the " Red Nightingale " slammed. The major stood alone in front of the barricade.

He felt how each of his movements was followed by hundreds of sharp, hate-filled eyes. He knew that he was the vanquished now. He had been treated like a schoolboy. Brazenly and full of scorn this woman had looked at him from the window just now, with no fear that he would draw his revolver and blow her brains out. He returned to the car.

" Start—back to the station ! "

At that moment the silence of the alley was broken by piercing shouts and boos. The windows flew open.

" Go to hell—you bloodhounds ! "

" Cowardly skunks ! "

" Red Front ! "

The alley almost burst under the screaming and scornful laughter of the men and women. Like a salvo of bursting shells the shouting and laughing tore the air and rang out over the bent heads of the police.

The furious but powerless roaring of the motors became softer. They had gone—withdrawn. Vanquished, without a shot, without the throwing of a single stone. One sole miserable barricade, thrown up in a hurry, had sufficed to fill them with panic. They had not been prepared for resistance.

A few minutes later the alley was again filled with people who tried to strengthen the barricade as quickly as possible. No one doubted that the police would return in a short time and storm the obstacle by armed force. But all felt at the same time that the red alley had just won a victory over the police.

.   .   .   .   .   .

Slowly the evening shadows fell on the houses.

In the room in the second backyard Anna prepared beds for the children as best she could, on the floor, with cushions and blankets. Hermann's little Heide crouched in a corner and whispered endearingly to her kitten. Without her pussy she would never have come here.

Anna placed the little ones side by side and tucked them in. They were tired with playing and crying. A little five-year-old girl from the front house wore a white bandage round her head. When the police had shot into the rooms during the afternoon she had been wounded on the forehead by a flying piece of mortar.

Anna opened the window and looked down into the dark water of the Panke, flowing slowly and noiselessly between dark walls. Here at the back all was perfectly quiet. The high houses deadened the noise of the alley. A few miserable little shrubs, with the first delicate green hue of young buds, grew on the banks. Spring came in late between these high sunless walls, where man and nature had to fight against filth and dirt for their existence.

She felt the soft evening wind on her hot face. It is already May, she was thinking. . . . Outside in the large gardens of the suburbs it will soon be summer. Then the foul smell would again penetrate their dwellings. Wearily she laid her head against the window frame. The soft, warm air caressed her forehead, her neck and her hands. Outside the window a bird was hopping in the sand, a grey miserable-looking sparrow.

The strong scent of the May wind which suddenly mingled with the foul smell of the water, discomfited her. It was a heavy, sickly smell of decay, such as sometimes comes from ivy and tombstones and makes the heart heavy and oppressed.

A rat jumped into the water with a soft plonk, rippling the surface in its wake.

CHAPTER V

THE STORMING OF THE "RED NIGHTINGALE"

SHORTLY after seven o'clock it became known in the alley that Fröbius the shopkeeper in the Kolberger-strasse only a few minutes off had been shot in the mouth and killed by a policeman under the railway bridge. In the Antonstrasse they had shot down the war invalid Reitnack outside a restaurant into which he had tried to escape. He had bled to death on the pavement. They had fired at everyone who tried to bring help. Erna Zielke, aged fifteen, had been severely wounded by a shot in the thigh. Report after report reached the " Red Nightingale." Dead, wounded, beaten down, arrested, men, women, children ! Every fresh report strengthened the determination to defend the alley and the lives of its inhabitants at all costs. It had become immaterial to what political creed they subscribed individually. The workers had become free targets, the president had given liberty to each police-man to shoot and baton whom he pleased. In number 6 they had fired through the windows into the flat of the Social Democrat Hainen.

" This is a punitive expedition against the alley ! " called out old Hübner. He had been one of the first to help in building the barricades.

" They know that this street is the red heart of Wedding," someone said as he lifted his nickel spectacles in his hand.

" Hallo ! . . . Comrade speaker," Kurt called out and clapped the pale young comrade heartily on the shoulder. " Fine, that you have come ! "

The others also greeted the speaker and the young man was glad that they regarded him as one of themselves in

115

this dangerous situation and did not show any suspicion towards him. For after all he was a stranger here, unknown to all except the members of the street cell who had heard him speak at the last meeting in the " Red Nightingale."

A quarter of an hour later, several couriers reported that the police had begun to surround the district. They had shot a courier, a young fifteen-year-old worker from his cycle near the Nettelbeckplatz. Heavy wound in the back. He would scarcely pull through.

It began to get dark. The shopkeepers in the Reinicken-dorfer-strasse had placed sheets of iron in front of their shop windows. In the pubs all the heavy wooden blinds except those outside the entrances had been lowered. Again and again the surrounding streets were filled with workers who formed demonstrations and marched to the centre of the town.

Shots cracked in the distance.

It began at the Wiesenstrasse corner of the alley. Stones crashed into the street lamps whose glass panes fell to the ground with a loud clatter. Lamp after lamp was extinguished. At the top of the gas pipe a small blue flame burned between the broken panes. These the workers kept burning to prevent the gas from escaping. As far as the old-fashioned type of low lamps were concerned, young fellows simply climbed up and turned the gas off. The ring of darkness spread further and further around the barricades, so that soon only large, clumsy silhouettes were visible in the faint blue light of the approaching night.

About eight o'clock shots cracked from the Nettelbeck-platz and soon came nearer. The rolling noise of heavy police lorries in rapid motion. Excited shouts rang through the alley. Doors slammed. The lights in the windows went out. The blinds of the " Red Nightingale " rattled down in front of the windows. Someone ran across the street and disappeared in a cellar entrance. Then all was quiet.

Empty and grey the alley lay silent behind the barricade. The motionless air smelt of spring and poverty. . . .

Noiselessly a broad, white floodlight swept across the

empty space from the corner of the Pankstrasse. Like a cold finger of light it crept haltingly up the house walls, along the entire alley.

Everything was in deathly silence. Only the white, hard light ate its way up the walls and strayed to the roofs above, shrouded in the first shadows of a starless night. Then the floodlight was pointed directly at the wide, high barricade. Behind it lay the enemy.

It was so quiet that the low, sharp command came like a sharp iron missile. Hundreds of shadows crouched down and the piercing sound of a rifle fusilade shook the air. The echo reverberated from the walls and rolled on through all the streets of Wedding.

The game had started. Salvo after salvo rang out. A stone smashed the searchlight. A few convulsive flashes—then the white eye was dark. Like dancing sparks the fire flamed from the mouths of the carbines. Whirring, the leaden bullets crashed against the walls of the houses from which the plaster fell heavily to the ground. They hit the sheet-iron sides of the dust-bins with a loud boom, ricocheted from the heavy iron in a sort of cross-fire. The whole alley seemed like a grey, motionless monster whose gigantic body had to be pierced thousands of times, before it would stop breathing.

Suddenly the loud shriek of a woman came from one of the houses. It was swallowed up by the incessant noise of the guns. The same moment a second searchlight flared up from the Reinickendorfer-strasse on the other side. Its vibrating ray revealed blue clouds of dust and powder smoke above the barricade.

The police attacked from both sides at once. They shot at each other across the barricade without, in their mad fright, noticing what they were doing. Each side believed the shots to be those of the enemy.

The dark shadow of a man ran at a crouch through the triangle of the barricade. Suddenly he stopped, bent forward, tore open his jacket and collapsed gurgling. Then there was silence.

He lay quite alone on the asphalt between the three

barricades over which the bullets swept from both sides. From a smashed window above someone had noticed. It was the same window through which the shining barrel of a repeater was now protruding.—A short flash of fire— Peng ! It was the first shot fired from the alley !

Behind the window stood Thomas, who, till now, had taken the arms from everybody carrying them. His face was as calm as ever, as he drew his hand with the revolver back a little, aimed and shot again, aimed and shot. It contained six bullets. Then he reloaded with his bandaged hand, went to the window in the adjoining room and shot again. Only once did he turn when he heard someone who had rushed into the dark room, and was calling for him. An unattached young worker.

At that moment the white searchlight fixed the wall of the room and fell on the terrified face of the young man. One—two seconds, then it swept on. Mad fear was marked on the distorted mouth of the boy.

" Shoot . . . you cur ! " shouted Thomas. " Like this . . . see ? "   Peng . . . peng . . . peng. . . . He emptied the drum through the broken window.

" Emil of number 5 is lying down there . . . do you hear ? . . . *Now the time has come.* . . . Boys . . . all who have guns must use them . . . otherwise we are finished. . . ."   A bullet bounced from the edge of the wall in front of him amidst a shower of plaster and hit the ceiling with a crack. He turned round, somewhat calmer.

" Where is Kurt Zimmermann ? Where is Paul ? "

" In number 3, I think."

" You go there—climb over the wall in the yard—you understand ! and tell them : not to stop anyone—who——"

" Am . . . bu . . . lance ! "   From the flat above his a woman screamed out of the window.

" Whoever has anything must *shoot !* "   The boy ran out of the room.

.   .   .   .

The police in the Pankstrasse passed over to the attack. The firing on the windows and the alley was intensified. Under its cover the police stormed forward. Helmets and nickel buttons glittered from the entrance of the alley. They rushed towards the barricades, firing ceaselessly. From the other side the police who could not get a clear view of the situation fired across the barricade at their own colleagues. Stones flew out of the dark windows. Shouting and shooting the police jumped on to the barricade fully prepared for a hand-to-hand struggle. The barricade was—empty!

"Cursed swine!"

A stone tore up the face of an East Prussian peasant boy. "Damned curs!" he wiped the blood from his face. The locks of the rifles clanked continuously. Go on banging at that invisible red monster! If only one had an aim!

The narrow black point of an officer's boot turned the man over who was lying a motionless lump on the ground between the beams. The belly was black and moist like the dark spot on the asphalt.

From the passage next to the "Red Nightingale" revolver fire flared up. Butt ends of rifles crashed against the blinds of the pub.

"Forward," the officer shouted ". . . they're inside there!"

The door to the "Red Nightingale" crashed to pieces. The police knew that here was the communist stronghold of the Köslin quarter.

"Hands up—get out, all of you!" The major's torch swept the dark room. It was—empty!

"Bloody gang!" Someone turned the switch of the electric light. Tack went the switch, but remained dark. Torches came out. Chairs and tables were overturned. On the wall was a newspaper page headed : "Fighting May Day, 1929." A policeman cursed and tore down the front page of the *Rote Fahne*. They found no one.

Black and uncanny the passage leading to the hall in the back opened before them. The new men did not know the interior of the pub. The major discovered the passage and stormed through it with raised revolver. A kick opened the door at the end. There was a light behind. The

room seemed empty. But in one corner two youngsters
were sitting and playing—cards !

The glass door leading to the yard stood open. Their
quarry had vanished ! Again disappearing, silently and
without a trace, diving into unknown hiding-places
swallowed up by the darkness of the passages and yards. . . .

A few empty cartridges was all they found. As for the
two youths who had " played cards "—nothing in their
pockets but a few buttons, a piece of string, cigarettes and
a dirty handkerchief. No evidence of any kind, no membership cards of the " Rote Frontkämpferbund " (the Red
Front Fighters' League) or the Young Communist League—
nothing but two young, unmoved faces suffering with
tightly closed lips the terrible manhandling of the police.

No one dare enter the dark and silent yard . . .

Outside the " Red Nightingale " the policemen tore
down the barricades in the glare of a searchlight and under
the cover of a special detachment which, stationed on both
sides of the street, fired uninterruptedly into the windows.
The black holes in the grey walls were the countless sharp
and fearful eyes of the monster—the red alley ! Still living
and breathing, inaccessible, like some great monster of old,
invincible, though bleeding from a hundred wounds. The
heart,—the red heart of Wedding—hammered on, stronger
and wilder than the barking rifles of the police.

When the searchers pulled away a dust-bin a small,
dirty hand fell to the ground. Over the hanging head they
saw a grey overall sleeve. They cleared away boards and
beams and flashed their torches into the white, young face
of a sixteen-year-old worker. Above the left eye there
was a dark round hole, from which a thin stream of blood,
now dried up, ran over knitted brows. The mouth small
as a young girl's.

In the sand beside him the policemen found a small
shining rifle and a little heap of percussion caps.

The torch went out. . . .

.   .   .   .

The barricade was taken, but not the alley. The dark
crevice between the high houses seemed impregnable.

With difficulty a passage had been made between the barricades on the road. The police retreated. The sound of their nailed boots was replaced by a hard clanging rattle from the Reinickendorfer-strasse. A powerful search-light lit up the alley like daylight, making dark fleeting shadows. At the same moment a machine-gun commenced firing. Through the ruins of the barricade a heavy armoured car pushed its way.

The attack on the alley !

Tack . . . tack . . . tack . . . tack. . . . The shining white steel-coated bullets sang and whistled the song of law and order. Stones and bullets shot from miserable, rusty, small-calibre pistols jumped ineffectively off the steel plates. The fire-spitting fortress rolled on and on. Some yards behind it followed the police—the best, the bravest, the youngest, the most brutal, in extended line.

And then the game began. Every house, passage, yard was to be captured. At the point of the rifles women and children were turned out of bed, the mattresses searched, cupboards and rooms. Shadows flying in deadly terror on the stairs were hunted to attics, hounded down, batoned to the ground, mauled and arrested. But in most cases invisibility had again swallowed the men they sought.

" There has been shooting from your rooms ! "

" Yes. Look at the wall. You can see your own bullets."

" Hold your tongue !—Where have you hidden those dogs ? Eh . . . ? "

" Look for yourself . . . " the women replied mockingly. They knew that the police would not dare to push further into the alley. Let them tear up the floors of the houses near the barricades if they wanted to. They would find bugs and beetles, but not our men. . . .

. . . . . .

At that moment the telephone rang in the room of the commander of the Berlin Police at Alexanderplatz.

Paul had tried to pick up connection with the outside by telephone from a shop during the attack. Everywhere the responsible party functionaries were engaged, in street work, at meetings or elsewhere. At last he got through to the parliamentary fraction of the party and gave— shots were cracking outside—a short report of the situation in the alley.

Paul did not know that at the same time the streets of Neukölln were being defended by the workers in the same way with barricades against the armoured cars of the police. He did not know that the Police President had long ago turned down the demand of the fraction to withdraw the police troops at once from the beleaguered workers' quarters. Paul was still firmly convinced that this attack on the alley was an irresponsible act of the officers in charge, without the knowledge of the centre.

On the strength of his report, deputy M. made a renewed attempt at about 10 o'clock at night to get into touch with the police presidium, in order to demand the withdrawal of the police.

The deputy commander, Colonel Hellriegel, answered the telephone.

" Are you aware of what is happening at the present moment in the Köslinerstrasse, colonel ? Are you aware of the fact that there is no longer any kind of street fight, but a senseless butchering of the inhabitants, such as we've not seen since the time of the Anti-Socialist Laws ? We demand that you give orders for the immediate withdrawal of your troops ! "

" I am exceedingly sorry, sir, but Commander Heimannsberg left a quarter of an hour ago to take personal charge of the situation, and without his instructions I am powerless to do anything in this matter."

" In that case you must get into touch with the Commander immediately."

" I shall do so. Please call again in twenty minutes."

Twenty minutes . . . ! It was ghastly to think of what could happen in that space of time ! How many people would still be shot . . . ? The Police President had given the officers full power and everyone in Berlin knew that for the present they would not dream of giving up that power again. Now at last they had achieved their heart's desire. The workers had been chased, battered to the ground, shot down like mad dogs and provoked, until they had begun to hit back. The " putsch " was in sight ! And suddenly to stop everything just at this moment ? Never ! A bourgeois journalist who desired to speak with his personal acquaintance, Major L. over the telephone at the presidium, received the reply : " The major is engaged at the front ! "

The Berlin police officers waiting in the room of the Police President were full of the fighting spirit of war-time. They were intoxicated with the spirit of the offensive. The Vice-President who " did not think at all," was absent on leave. To preserve his easy conscience he had fled from the scene of action. . . .

After twenty minutes the telephone rang : " Well, colonel ? "

" I am in the position to inform you, sir, that the police have been withdrawn from the Köslinerstrasse. Everything is quiet in that street. But will you now please exert your influence to prevent any further attacks on the police ? "

" Colonel, the workers have not disturbed the peace once to-day or attacked the police of their own accord. We have merely demanded the right of demonstrating on the 1st of May, as the workers have done for the past forty years. Nothing more ! The workers have not commenced hostile action against the police once to-day—but you will find that their patience has a limit ! "

The suspicion of the parliamentary fraction was verified a few minutes later. They were informed by telephone that the police far from having withdrawn from the alley even for a few minutes, was raging in it as before. The police report had been pure deception.

· · · · · ·

Not till many hours afterwards did the situation calm down in the Köslinerstrasse and the Neukölln fighting areas.

CHAPTER VI

THE NIGHT WHEN NO ONE SLEPT . . .

TOWARDS two in the morning the comrades met in the " Red Room." Stray shots were still heard from time to time in the neighbourhood. Hanging from a nail on the cupboard, Hermann's oil-lamp shone on the tired dirty faces in the smoke-filled room.

Sitting in the shadow on the edge of the bed, Anna watched Kurt who was writing at the table. Now and then he looked up thoughtfully and then wrote down a new line in his slow, uneven hand.

In the " Red Room " only the scratching of the pen was to be heard.

Paul came in last. Otto represented the Young Communists, broad-shouldered, big and good-humoured in his calmnesss, as usual. He touched the brown teddy bear hanging from the ceiling with his finger and smiled when it began to swing with paws stretched downward. Paul looked furiously at him and stopped the swinging of the bear. Thomas crouched on a stool smoking. Behind him stood three other workers of the street cell.

Kurt broke the silence : " Comrades, we must dispatch a reliable courier. I have written a short report and compiled a list of the dead and wounded . . . it must be sent at once ! "

Thomas raised his head and the lamplight fell on his tired, relaxed face.

" How many ? "

" Five dead . . . till now . . . but I don't know whether that's all ! " A suppressed sound came from the bed.

" I think we should not give any names at present,"

Kurt went on. " Perhaps some of you know of others.
This is how I have put it :

    1 shot in the chest (Virchow Hospital).
    1 shot in the hand (Municipal Hospital).
    1 shot in the hand (Virchow Hospital).
    1 shot in the chest (dead).
    1 shot in the cheek (Virchow Hospital).
    1 shot in the hand (at home).
    1 shot in the foot (at home).
    1 shot in the knee (at home).
    1 woman shot in the stomach (Virchow Hospital).
    1 shot in the head (dead).
    1 shot in the ankle (Jewish Hospital).
    1 shot through both legs (Fire Station).
    1 shot in the chest (dead).
    1 shot in the foot (at home).
    2 shot through the leg (at home).
    1 woman shot in the arm (at home).
    1 shot in the head (dead).
    1 badly wounded through the bite of a police dog
       (at home).

The others I don't know of . . . but I am sure there
are more. . . ."

When she saw Kurt's changed face, Anna started. It
had suddenly gone grey ! He held out his list to the others,
but no one took it. It seemed as if they were afraid to take
the report in their hands thereby accepting it as a concrete
fact.

Their ears still resounded with the hammering of the
machine-gun, the shouting of the people, the cries of pain of
those who had been bludgeoned, the cracking of rifles and
revolvers. . . .

They had fought and hit back, because they had been
provoked at the point of cold steel—nothing more ! And
this terrible list was the result.

Behind the glittering helmets, among the white, cold
faces of the dead, they began to understand the political
face of the events of May 1st, 1929.

It was essential now that they should see clearly. The

situation had developed beyond the narrow sphere of the alley. The instinctive feeling of proletarian responsibility on which they had acted, required a political consciousness. Above all the question burnt in their minds : What would happen to-morrow ?

One of the workers took the report and without a word went out.

Thomas looked at his watch and said : " Comrades, it is now half-past two ; we must be finished in less than an hour at the latest. I propose that Kurt gives a short report and that we then decide what is to be done."—He turned deliberately to Kurt. As soon as he saw Paul's dejected face he knew that it would be a mistake to count on him to-day.

But Kurt was a changed man from henceforward. His clumsy movements had become hard and determined ; all his thoughts were concentrated on essentials and on the next step. The builder's labourer, Kurt Zimmermann was one of those proletarians who in unforeseen emergencies become revolutionary leaders, without knowing it themselves.

A quarter of an hour earlier, Kurt had been sitting alone in this room attempting to analyse the terrible events, and to derive a clear-cut line of action from them. He knew that as long as Hermann was absent the political responsibility rested on his shoulders. He did not require formal recognition to see this.

" Comrades," Kurt opened the discussion, " we have bad communication with other party centres. It is perfectly clear that none of our comrades had counted on this development. Nor had we. But I have found a newspaper on Hermann's table which proves that other people saw clearly what would happen." He took up a newspaper and held it close to the lamp :

" The first of May—Berlin's Day of Death,—that is the headline," he explained, " . . . it is easy to put the blame for the suffering which the 1st of May will bring to many workers' families on the shoulders of the Communists ; all that need be said is that the Communists should not have called demonstrations as long as the ban was enforced. But it is useless to fight for the *murderer* who has consciously violated the thousand-year-old commandment ' Thou shalt not kill.' What is the use of demanding his pardon, if one can look on in cold blood, and see how all preparations are made to shoot down workers who violate an order of the Police President Zörgiebel of 1929 ? . . . It is a matter for the concern of the whole party, when the lives of workers are to be sacrificed for the maintenance of state authority."

" Man, where was that printed ? " Thomas called out excitedly and jumped to his feet.

" This was printed in the social democratic " Sächsische Volksblatt " on the 19th of April," Kurt answered calmly.

" Berlin's Day of Death . . ." Paul called out, " . . . that's true—they knew it beforehand . . . ! "

" This ought to be duplicated and distributed throughout Wedding ! "

" Of course we must bring out leaflets. Now were a paying for the lack of our own duplicator in the street cell ! I should think that the Party Centre will do something, but who can tell whether they'll be able to get anything through to us to-morrow ? But—let's first deal with the other point, I don't think there can be any more convincing proof for our claim that the police are responsible for all this than this S.P.D. paper. Even if the political reason is not given— for on that point the " left " S.P.D. are of one opinion with the others. But more important for us at this moment is the question : What will happen to-morrow ? "

There was an abrupt knock at the door . . . then again loud and impatiently.

" Who's that ? " The workers looked uneasily at one another.

" Light out," whispered Thomas.

Kurt extinguished the lamp. As they sat in the dark room they all knew one thing : if that's the police, every-thing is finished ! They heard someone calling on the stairs.

" That's not the police," Otto called out reassured.

Cursing he stumbled over the gas meter in the dark narrow passage.

" Who's there . . . ? "

" Open the door, this is Fritz ! "   Otto opened.

" What's the matter, Fritz ? " he asked while still in the dark passage.

" What is the matter—?   They're taking arms from the shop at the corner ! "

" What—who's getting arms ? "

" Well, not the police—you idiot ! "

Otto felt his way back through the dark flat. They had lighted the lamp again.

" Come on, boys ! " he said beaming " . . . they are clearing out the arms shop on the corner."   His eyes sparkled.   " Fine spirit in those boys.   While we are talking, they get on with the job."

Kurt looked so flabbergasted that Anna burst out laughing.

" I don't know what there is to laugh about," he flared up.   At bottom he was only annoyed that he had not thought of this himself.   Of course—one had to think of to-morrow.   And who knows what will develop in the next few days.   Moreover they were quite clear politically now.

" Well, comrades, let's go down quickly and see what they are doing ! "

.   .   .   .   .   .

The street was pitch black.   A fresh night wind met the workers.   Here and there dark shadows were to be seen outside the houses.   In the black doorways cigarettes glowed.   The men were talking in whispers to one another. No one could sleep that night.

Kurt and the other comrades hurried through the quiet dark street to the Pankstrasse.   At the corner a large red sign was visible above the heavy blinds : " Cutlery and Steel Goods."   On the street side everything was perfectly quiet.   But standing in front of the shop they heard muffled noises.

Through the house door they went into the backyard.

" Who's there ? " The call came from a hidden corner in the wall. Thomas answered.

Noiselessly a few shadows were climbing out of the back window carrying parcels. They worked quickly and without a sound. There was not much to take. It was not a real arms shop, its stock being mostly scissors, knives and razors. One man stood on guard in the shop to see that nothing was taken but potential weapons. There were small arms, Brownings, daggers and some knuckledusters. Better than nothing.

In less than a quarter of an hour the job was finished. Some arms were hidden in a safe place the others distributed to well-known, reliable workers, and in this, party membership had long ceased to be a decisive factor. Behind this defence stood the whole alley.

.   .   .   .   .   .

In the police station and emergency quarters the situation had completely changed.

To-night it was not Sergeant Schlopsnies who was standing at the window of station 95 looking with excited anticipation across to the Köslinerstrasse, but Wüllner, gazing into the dark shadows of the backyards.

He had taken part in that evening's fighting and had seen the dead youth with the tiny, half-open mouth, by the barricade. And ever afterwards he had been unable to get rid of the thought of the small white patch he had seen moving on the barricade shortly before the attack. When the searchlight from the other side shone directly behind the white patch, Wüllner had aimed carefully and fired. He had been excited, frightened, like all the others, at this dark uncanny street, and in that state of mind he had fired . . .

Perhaps it was merely a fixed idea of his overstrained brain. But the moment he flashed his torch into the white young face the thought settled in his mind that it had been his own bullet which had torn the black round hole over the left eye. Police Sergeant Wüllner—himself father of three children—was a murderer . . .

He did not hear his colleagues boasting about their brave

deeds in the room behind him trying to drown in harsh voices the fears that beset them. The spirit of the offensive had vanished in those East Prussian peasant boys. The greater their fear, the more brutal they had been. Something unknown, mysterious, powerful—the masses—had confronted them !

The door leading to the room of the lieutenant was torn open : " Sergeant Wüllner wanted by the major ! " Wüllner swung round startled at the sound of his name. " What do they want of me ? " Did they know that he was a murderer . . . did they want to take him to account . . . had somebody seen him ? Nonsense—more than one had been shot . . . according to orders . . .

He fastened his collar, and as he passed, his comrades became silent. Wüllner had been called for, because something was to happen again—or so they were thinking. He was the leader of the special patrol car—the SPAT car as they called it. If only they were not going to be sent out again in the dark . . .

Wüllner closed the door behind him and attempted to stand at attention. At the table in front of him were four officers, Major Beil, Captain von Malzahn, Major v. d. Branitz who had been wounded by his own men in the attack, and a young lieutenant whom Wüllner did not know. The young policemen from Brandenburg said that he was from the Reichswehr. But they did not know for certain. The floor under the table was covered with cigarette ends and ashes.

" Come a little closer, Wüllner," demanded the major, " those outside need not hear everything. Right. Now, Wüllner, you are the most reliable here. We have a special order for you."

At this moment a complete change came over Wüllner. " I am the most reliable because I have killed a human being," he was thinking . . . and now they had a new job for him . . . he was to do something like that again. . . . No. . . . He would refuse . . . he was not reliable ! A wild disgust possessed him. He felt his knees trembling with excitement.

"What is the matter with you?" The major looked at him in astonishment.

"Watch your nerves, man!—You will now run through the district in the SPAT car and report all you see! Shoot at everything that crosses your path. Understand! If you need any extra men select a few reliable fellows yourself. Do this thing properly.—Now go!"

But Wüllner did not go. He still stood on the same spot and looked at the major.

"Did you hear my command?" the major asked softly with a dangerous note in his voice.

"Yes, sir!"

"Then what are you waiting for?"

Yes, what was Wüllner waiting for? He stared at the face of his superior. Gradually his fingers tightened. He pressed the nails into the palms of his hands. Now, now he had made up his mind; now he had to speak. He wanted to scream, to shout, but he could only stammer softly and helplessly:

"Sir, it is—impossible for me."

The major's face went purple. "Impossible?" he shouted.

"Yes," Wüllner replied, "it is impossible. I have— murdered a human being."

"Pardon, sir," Captain von Malzahn intervened, "I believe the man has lost his nerve completely. He doesn't know what he is saying."

The major silenced Malzahn with a gesture. He went round the table to Wüllner who was still standing motionless, as if rooted to the ground and walking close up to the pale sergeant, blew the smoke of his cigarette straight into his face, hissing like a snake: "Coward!" He spat the word into the ashen face of the policeman.

"Get out—you swine, you bolshevik—get out, quickly!" he roared. The officers rose from their seats.

Behind the door the conversation of the men which began again when Wüllner went into the major's room, suddenly broke off.

It took some time for Wüllner to grasp how he was being

humiliated by the officer. He only knew that if he now opened his mouth he would burst out. He could not control himself any longer :

" It's murder, you are committing, murder, murder ! I'm no coward. I've been serving for ten years. Never been a coward. No more of this for me—no more, no more ! "

Before the officers could prevent him, he grasped the carbine leaning against the wall and crashed it at the major's feet.

That night he was taken to the police presidium under arrest.

From another station in Wedding, three other policemen of the emergency detachment who had been taken from the Maikäfer barracks in the Chausseestrasse were arrested and taken away.

CHAPTER VII

A MAN WALKS THROUGH THE TOWN

WHEN the dawn of the 2nd of May broke, Kurt left the alley. It was only to be expected that the district would be cut off again presently and so the immediate task was to establish connections with the outside world ; to see what was the general opinion in town about yesterday's events ; and to collect some information for the people in the alley. Men gathered in front of the newspaper stalls on their way to work. They snatched the papers, wet from the press, out of the hands of the vendors.

"Blood Guilt of the Communists" screamed the *Vorwärts* in black headlines on the front page. "Moscow needs corpses!" That was the *Volksblatt* of the "left" S.P.D. The workers laughed scornfully : the same lefts who previously had called the Police President the May Day "murderer." The Communist baiters revelled in orgies. No bourgeois paper could rival the lies and calumnies of the Social Democratic newspapers. "The ponce as demonstrator," was the heading of a leading article in one of them. Kurt read out the juiciest bits to workers round him on Wedding station : "Freedom to demonstrate exists, but not for the scum and those people who have only succeeded in demonstrating that they have forfeited their political rights in Berlin and can only be dealt with as criminals."

An old Social Democratic worker tore the newspaper from his hand, his face red with fury, threw it to the ground and trampled on it. "Swine, those swine," he shouted again and again. "Mates—am I a ponce ? Are we scum ? "

133

A slogan which appeared in different variations in all the S.P.D. newspapers had been issued by the Social Democratic press service. It was : " Moscow needs corpses ! "

Feverishly Kurt tried to read all the newspapers he could lay hands on. He could not buy all of them. Where he saw a man standing with a newspaper he went up to him and begged him to let him see it for a moment. " Sheer madness ! " he thought again and again. There aren't as many lies as all this. He always looked first at the reports on the fighting in the alley.

In one paper the attack of the police on the barricade in front of the " Red Nightingale " was described like this : " . . . On the word of command about 150 Communists stormed out of the surrounding houses and erected a barricade six foot high out of lorries, builders' vans, gas pipes, stones and beams across the street. The action was so well prepared that the police who appeared ten minutes later were received by a real fusilade. Behind the barricade about 100 Communists armed with army revolvers and rifles had taken position and opened a furious fire. Presently firing broke out in the rear of the police. The Communists had occupied attics and roofs from which they kept up an incessant fire. In a short space of time hundreds of volleys were fired. The weak police detachment had to withdraw for a few minutes to await reinforcements."

Kurt was breathless with amazement. When the police appeared for the first time not a shot had been fired. " Behind the barricade about 100 Communists armed with army revolvers and rifles had taken position." Behind the barricade two were lying dead when the attack began. Was it they who had fired the salvoes ?

He became more and more confused. Who had written this ? He turned the paper round—the *Vorwärts*—— Like a bear, raving with fever, Kurt stumbled through town. When he saw a policeman he trembled with hatred.

He did not understand all this. Why did the people walk about calmly and as if nothing had happened ? The trams ran as usual. The trains rolled over the bridges under which Kurt was standing, and the thundering noise of the iron girders was music to him in the unbearable silence of the morning.

It ought to crash, everything ought to crash, to break. Why don't the workers smash the printing machines that spew out these lies, why do they just talk and swear and then go on to their factories as usual?

At the Oranienburgertor there was the branch office of a newspaper. People were standing in front of the windows reading the morning editions which were hung out. Workers, a tram driver in uniform with his bag under his arm, prostitutes who had found no clients that night, night club visitors with tightly buttoned-up overcoats, smelling of cigarettes and beer. Kurt pushed his way to the window. He did not hear someone swearing behind him. He started to read, anywhere, in the middle of the page: " Even if due allowance is made for the strained nerves of the overworked police and officers, the ruthless handling of the baton is open to grave criticism. The punishment of whipping was abolished from our penal code largely because it brutalized the officials. The police have re-introduced it and the result is that they apparently enjoy beating what comes under their hands. Pedestrians who had nothing whatever to do with the demonstration and whose presence was a sheer accident, were roughly handled by the police. Anyone who protested to a police officer would be told (this actually happened at the corner of the Turm and Stromstrasse in Moabit) 'We are not Jews, we don't negotiate.' The baton is used readily. If the questioner did not retire in great haste, he received a blow on the head."

Kurt looked at the head of the paper, a bourgeois journal. The first voice raising a timid protest against the police. Oh, how stupidly written, he thought, " roughly handled " — that idiot should have been with us in Wedding.

" Man, we didn't notice anything of that sort in the ' White Mouse,' " a fat, oily voice croaked behind him. He turned and stood in a cloud of alcohol-infested breath, stale smoke and disgusting penetrating scent.

" Well, what's the matter, my man ? " The speaker was

corpulent, rubicund, a bowler hat was tipped on one side
of his head and a white withered flower stuck in his buttonhole. The old roué and the tired worker stood face to face.
A glare of hatred shining from blood-shot eyes disturbed
the night bird. His drink-sodden brain did not grasp what
he saw, but this stare made him feel uneasy, spoiled his
feeling of saturated content.

"What's the matter?" His growl was unpleasant and
touched with a suspicious aloofness. He put his hand in
his pocket and took out a handful of loose money.

"Here you are, fellow, go get yourself a beer!" He
held out a piece of money to him. Kurt saw the silver coin
lying on the flabby palm. Next moment he brushed it
away like vermin. With a hard clink the money fell on
the pavement. A woman bent down and picked it up.

Speechless, head down, he pushed his way through the
people and went on. "Scum!" he murmured and took a
deep breath of the fresh morning air to rid himself of the
drunkard's disgusting smell.

.   .   .   .   .   .

The *Rote Fahne* was sold out everywhere. The
workers were not the only ones who had waited for it.

Kurt ran through the Elsässerstrasse. The nearer he
came to the Bülowplatz, the more frequently he saw red
flags flying from the windows. Here lived workers.

A heavy lorry filled with police rushed by. They had
rifles in their hands, and a machine gun peeped from under
the last bench. Pale, haggard faces. Kurt's blood
hammered in his temples.

At the Rosenthaler Tor no papers whatever were to be
had. The smell of warm soup came from a restaurant. He
suddenly remembered that he had had his last meal
yesterday morning. Later, later—he was too excited now!
A lorry piled with vegetable baskets rolled across the
Bülowplatz from the market. People were standing
talking outside the shops. A number of workers were
crossing the empty square. Behind the sandstone block
of the " Volksbühne " was the " Karl-Liebknecht-Haus,"
the central offices of the Communist Party. On the tower

a big red flag waved, at half mast. In the street crowds of workers stood in front of the red show-cases reading the *Rote Fahne* :

" Out of the factories !
Political mass strike against the murderers of the workers !
Down with Zörgiebel !—Lift the state of siege !
Free the class war prisoners !—Punish the murderers !
" Call special meetings at once in all factories ! Declare for strike action ! Elect delegates ! Representatives of all factories, delegates, factory council members, meet to-night at 8 o'clock for the general Greater Berlin delegate conference in the Sophien Hall. No factory must remain unrepresented."

" Ten dead and 150 wounded !—Proletarian Berlin downs tools ! Berlin's factories are surging seas to-day. There is not one social democratic worker who would dare to defend the terrible blood bath caused by Zörgiebel. Again and again boundless indignation and fury bursts forth. It finds expression in heated conversation, in the demand for the immediate declaration of a political mass strike."

" In the meantime the workers are beginning to leave work spontaneously. On the Karstadt building on the Hermannplatz the workers refused to start their work this morning. The Police President must go. That is the unanimous demand of the Berlin proletariat."

" The plumbers and labourers of the firm Voltz & Co., building the Eden Hotel, and the plumbers and labourers working in the Dublinerstrasse downed tools this morning in a unanimous protest against this appalling murder of workers."

" The workers employed by the firm Jacobowitz, Karlplatz, raise the strongest protest and call upon the German workers to enter immediately on a political mass strike, with the demand of the dissolution of the entire Social Democratic police régime."

" The men of the firm of Holzmann, Ltd., passed a

resolution in a factory meeting at which 500 were present
to strike immediately in protest against the May Day
blood bath. Singing the ' International ' the proletarians
left work. The task workers in the Volkspark went on
strike. Follow these examples ! "

"Hamburg, 2nd May (*From our special correspondent*) :
"The workers of the Reihersteg-Werft have declared a
24-hours' protest strike. Almost all S.P.D. and Reichsbanner members are taking part. . . ."

Kurt stood among the workers and read and read, till
the letters seemed to dance. His weary and inflamed eyes
burned. But for the first time he felt calm, quite calm. Now
he knew everything was in order ! Last night had not been
in vain.

As he turned and went slowly back across the square he
felt ashamed of the terrible fear which had overcome him.
He had been ridiculous he thought, indignant with himself.
On the way here he had heard workers swearing at the
Communists, believing all the lying newspapers wrote,
believing that only thieves and rogues had fought in the
Köslinerstrasse and in Neukölln. He had feared that all
might think the same. Now he saw that it was the old
tactics of the S.P.D. and the bourgeoisie to describe all
really revolutionary workers as down-and-outs and
criminals whenever there was a real class fight, in order to
prevent the united action of the whole working-class.

Now with this inner calmness he relaxed. He felt how
tired and hungry he was. It was really a psychological
reaction. He took the next tram back to the alley.

.   .   .   .   .   .

In countless factories and works protest meetings were
held in the course of the day. The cigarettes works
Manoli, Massary and Josetti with 2500 male and female
workers was the first large factory to declare a protest
strike, the transformer works, Ober-Schöneweide, with
2300 workers, unanimously followed the instructions of
the red May Day committee. The North German Ball-
bearing Works joined. At 3 o'clock in the afternoon the

workers of the Leiser shoe factory, mostly women, downed tools. The 400 shoe workers of the firm of Huta, Ltd., announced a protest strike for to-morrow.

The papers reported from the Ruhr area that leaflets on the events in Berlin had been distributed at all pit-heads in Bottrop and Osterfeld. The greater part of the workers stopped work at once and demanded the calling of a general strike. A factory council conference representing seventy-seven factories in Halle decided to call a twenty-four hours protest strike on Saturday. The miners of the large pit Thyssen III in Hamborn refused to enter the pit. At the Prosper II pit the workers enforced the closing of pits II and III. From all parts of the Reich came the news of protest strikes in works and factories. All the builders in Berlin were out. The workers in all five factories in one street joined in a common protest strike. On the evening of May 2nd, fifteen overcrowded mass meetings were held in the largest halls in Berlin. All street cells of the Party met. The " Rote Frontkämpferbund "* and the " Rote Jungfront "* called all their members together.

In the Reichstag after the S.P.D. and the other bourgeois parties had refused to discuss the May Day occurrences, the Communist fraction sang the " International " and broke up the sitting. Outside, in the streets of Berlin, the police were shooting.

During a protest demonstration in Neukölln three more workers were shot and twenty badly wounded. Reichswehr and artillery were mobilized and stood in preparation for the night. The fight went on.

* Red Front Fighting League and Red Young Front, proletarian self-defence organisations.

CHAPTER VIII

ANNA READS THE LAST CHAPTER

THOUSANDS of workers came to the alley in the afternoon from all parts of the town. The police did not dare to enter the district. Only " civil informers" were present—and they were in large numbers. The workers were in control of the areas far beyond the actual barricade both in Neukölln and in Wedding.

About this time Hermann returned. He hurried through the masses on the Nettelbeckplatz without pausing. There was no sign of the police. He went through the alley and saw the innumerable marks of shots on the houses. On the stairs he met Anna.

" Where are the comrades ? "

" A good thing that you have come, Hermann," said Anna in relief. " They're all at your place ! "

He went up the stairs. The kitchen was full of men and women. " Hallo, Hermann, thank goodness ! " Kurt greeted him, " Let's go to the ' Red Room ' at once ! "

Hermann asked how his wife and children were and then withdrew at once with the comrades into the " Red Room."

While Kurt was telling him in a few words what had happened, Hermann looked across several times to Paul who was sitting silently on a chair. Kurt did not mention his virtual replacement of Paul, but Hermann knew from Paul's expression. He heard how calmly and pointedly Kurt was speaking. He scarcely recognised the cement-heaver, formerly so shy. The night had altogether changed him.

Kurt had finished his report. " Have you spoken to the people on the street ? " Hermann asked. Kurt looked at him in astonishment. Damn it, no one had thought of that in the excitement. Hermann was annoyed. That was the most important thing just now, the few copies of the *Rote Fahne* which had reached the alley were insufficient to inform the masses about the real situation. Moreover the police had not allowed the newsboy with the *Rote Fahne* to pass the control in the morning.

" But none of us can speak properly." Kurt attempted to excuse their neglect. Hermann could not help laughing as he saw Kurt's depressed face. He remembered what they had done during the night. But, make a speech? No—-they were too scared for that!

A little later the strains of the "International" were heard in the alley. Hermann was standing on a dairy waggon and addressing the masses.

．　　．　　．　　．　　．　　．

The evening of May 2nd approached.

Nobody knew what the coming night, what the next few hours might bring. The press reports of the police presidium had been copied without criticism by the entire bourgeois press. Anyone who had not been a witness of the events in the alley or in Neukölln was bound to conclude after reading these reports that Berlin was in the midst of a " revolution " and that only the " victorious " advance of the police could stop it.

Thomas nearly choked with laughter when someone gave him a copy of the *Vorwärts* in the " Red Nightingale " which wrote that the Communists from their positions on the roofs, etc. " had shot 14 carbines to bits in the very hands of the police without even so much as a scratch to a single policeman." " By Jingo . . . that's what you call a perfect aim! We're all of us prize sharpshooters," he called out laughingly.

It seemed as if the police intended to fortify their courage with these lies, they had to magnify, distort, misrepresent everything. How else would anyone in Berlin have believed that in two small, rigorously surrounded areas, in Neukölln and in the alley in Wedding, a mere handful of workers armed with the most primitive weapons had been defending their streets and houses for thirty-six hours against about 14,000 policemen with the most up-to-date equipment, including heavy machine-guns, hand-grenades and armoured cars ?

Hermann had energetically contradicted Kurt's contention that they in the alley, isolated as they were, should never have taken up the fight in this way. Certainly the alley was poorly situated from the strategic point of view, that Hermann had to admit. It was too easily cut off. But, he said, fights of this kind would always develop first in localized slums such as these. In such quarters the defence would find the support of the entire population. The best proof of this were the struggles in Hamburg in 1923, which had been most successful in the " Gänge-Viertal," the slum district.

" You surely see yourself," Hermann pointed out to him, " that you could only have held out, because all the dwellings of the alley were at your disposal. As soon as the population sympathises with the workers and not with the police, the former have a certain definite amount of cover, while the latter are on enemy ground with every step they take."

They were standing in the dusky passage with the broken glass door which Kurt had slammed behind him when he escaped from the police yesterday.

Anna crossed the yard with the child. She and Kurt had seen one another only for a few minutes at rare intervals. From time to time she had appeared at his side, silently, without mentioning personal matters, until he was again called away somewhere. Not once, since the early morning of May 1st, had she tried to keep him back.

They had never so much as mentioned the critical moment of yesterday, when she had in all probability saved his life by calling to him. She was satisfied that he was still alive. Nothing else seemed of any importance just now. Why, she did not know. Her whole attitude was still purely emotional, like that of many women in the alley who had only been brought to the side of the workers by their hatred of the brutal police.

Kurt smiled at her, good-humouredly. " Come, Anna,

let's go to the square for a while—just to see what's happening there."

Kurt was anxious for the kid to stay at home, but Anna wanted to give him a breath of fresh air. Ever since yesterday morning he had been kept indoors with the other children.

.   .   .   .   .   .

It was already dusk. Here and there, groups of women were gossiping in the alley shops. In one shop the police bullet had shattered a cask of oil and its contents had run over the other foodstuffs, ruining them. Even from the street, Kurt and Anna could hear the excited argument as to who would pay damages. It was a heavy loss for small shopkeepers living from hand to mouth.

The big stores in the Reinickendorfer-strasse were nearly all closed or had their iron blinds down. Hundreds of people, among whom Kurt recognized many Social Democratic workers, were standing on the Nettelbeckplatz. Two women were sitting on a bench near the tram stop. Kurt heard in passing that one of them belonged to the S.P.D.; later he was informed that they were striking workers from the Manoli tobacco works.

From the peaceful aspect of the square one might almost conclude that no further dangers were threatening. But listening here and there to the conversation of the people Kurt realized that they were in a state of great fury and indignation which on the slightest provocation would break out into an uncontrollable storm.

News came that there had again been bloody collisions in other districts. The number of the dead now amounted to fifteen. The frequent and contradictory rumours only served to intensify the agitation. The police reports in the bourgeois papers and the evening edition of the *Vorwärts* were greeted with derisive laughter and boos. People had seen enough themselves!

Gradually, as the night descended, the faces of the people grew less distinct. It was cool. The yellow gas lamps began to shine.

Shortly after 10 o'clock the stormy meeting in the Pharus Halls ended.

An overflow meeting had also to be held outside in the courtyard. Hermann had put in an appearance, spoken briefly about the situation in the alley, and had disappeared again.

Along with the rest of the audience, Anna keeping close to Kurt, pushed her way towards the street, in order to get home again as quickly as possible. She herself now saw how silly it had been to bring the child with her.

While the crowd slowly pushed itself out, and she was speaking to Kurt of the excited course of the meeting, a wild pushing and shoving suddenly commenced. Kurt tried in vain to pull her out of the shouting and screaming throng. They were as if wedged in. He perceived policemen standing in the street in front of the out-streaming people.

An old worker attempted to speak to the Superintendent in Charge. Only the officer's excited face was to be seen. Rubber truncheon blows whistled down on the startled workers. A terrible panic arose !

The people ran—as far as it was at all possible to run in such a crowd—along both sides of the Mullerstrasse, chased by the wildly batoning policemen. The red face of a bawling policeman appeared right in front of Kurt. His cocked revolver was swung hither and thither amongst the crowd. Any second, and a shot might ring out.

Kurt did not ponder long. With his right arm he pushed Anna and the child behind him. His left fist shot out and hit the policeman right under the chin. As the policeman crumpled up, Kurt shouted something to Anna and disappeared amongst the crowd. The people ran on, over the body of the fallen policeman lying on the ground.

Anna pressed the boy closer and ran along the street with the weeping child.

Shots cracked behind her ! A young girl in front of her let out a sharp, thin scream. Someone picked her up, carried her with limp, hanging legs, into the lobby of a house.

Anna ran on. Her knees trembled. She staggered a few times but tore herself up again . . . further, only further. Close behind her shrilled a policeman's whistle. Somewhere a window-pane clattered to, and suddenly she saw nobody in front of her. Behind her she felt it cold and empty. She ran alone.

" Stand still " . . . shouted somebody. Heavy steps sounded closer—fainting, breathless, she ran on, staggering, swooning from fear and weakness. . . . A terrible blow thundered down on the back of her head. The skin drew together as in a sharp rending cramp. Her knees went weak. The straight line of the street lights heaved swimmingly before her eyes, and seemed to pour over her like a shaken-out sack of stones—the child slid out of her drooping arms.

She did not even feel the second blow. The lights receded in a deep, black shadow. With a sinister swiftness she sank down—into a dim, yawning abyss.—She no longer felt how the policeman tore her to her feet again and hauled her—her legs trailing along, to the police van, and threw her under a seat. The van was full.

" Back to the station ! " an officer shouted. His face was red with excitement. The policemen jumped on the running lorry, closing the shutters behind them. Then the car wheeled round sharply and rushed at full speed down the Müllerstrasse. Someone shouted from a window as it passed. A shot cracked against the wall of the house.

As they went down the pitch dark Weddingstrasse, the policemen bent almost to the floor of the van. At the tail, a policeman crouched behind a machine-gun. For the whole of the journey the leader of the squad took cover behind two of the prisoners who were sitting on the wooden bench with hands raised above their heads. The rattling and bumping of the van brought Anna slowly back to consciousness. An agonising pain at the back of her head restored full realisation of what had happened. On a level with her face was the black glossiness of a pair of top-boots, and between them the butt end of a carbine. She felt a stiffness in her arms. " My God, what can that be ? " she whispered.

The car dashed so sharply round a corner that her face was thrown against one of the boots. Terrified she pressed backwards. Pain still blurred her understanding. What had happened? What had become of Kurt? And the boy? For heaven's sake, where was the kid?

"Sergeant, sergeant—!" In her fright she had forgotten her pain and shouted to the policeman whose leather boots she clutched with both her arms.

"Cursed rat!" the policeman shouted as he jumped in terror. When, in the light of a passing gas lamp, he saw the deathly pale face of the woman under the bench, he kicked her and swore. "Hold your tongue." Her head fell back with a thud.

With a jolt the lorry stopped in front of the police station. Policemen came out of the lighted gateway. "Get off quickly!"

The prisoners jumped off the lorry and were driven like cattle into the building. "Close the windows!" a policeman shouted across the street. Seeing something move behind one of the windows in the second floor, he fired without further parley into the house across the way.

An elderly man stumbled against the pavement when he received a blow from behind. Someone beat him on the head. Howling with pain he fell against a policeman who gave him a blow with the butt end of his gun. He grasped the empty air with his hands and fell with a groan down the steps.

"Don't try on any monkey tricks here," a policeman called and forced him to his feet. Then they dragged him up with them.

Anna, who was the last one on the lorry, had witnessed the scene in horror. "No, no, I won't get down. You are going to beat us all to death," she shouted. She tried desperately to defend herself against the policeman who grasped her and pulled her down.

The screams and cries for help of those being beaten could be heard all the way down the street. "Close the door," called a sharp voice from the top of the stairs.

Then the beating continued. The newly arrested were driven upstairs.

They were driven with raised hands into the guardroom. Eleven workers—Anna the only woman among them.

The guardroom was packed with specials, young men, a strange excitement in their faces. They had been brought here as reinforcements a few hours ago.

" Ha,—so here are the barricade builders. Come here, my boy ! " A young policeman, of about twenty years old, struck a worker in the face with the palm of his hand. Bash ! another one as a welcome gift ! Ha ! that was a fine one! Why else did we learn this at the police school in Brandenburg ? But flesh is better than a leather ball. The swine is still on his feet ! Another blow on the left—above—bang. " Now, my boy, there you lie ! "

How easy it seemed ! It was like walking through a field and cutting off the heads of the thistles with a stick. The young police exulted in their strength and bravery.

" You are making me dirty." This one carefully wiped the blood off the edge of his sleeve with a handkerchief. His colleagues laughed hysterically.

" Come in. It's nice and warm here, you Muscovites ! "

Crack—bang—a prisoner fell with a groan against the wall.

" You swine, so you want to fly sky high . . . " A young worker collapsed at the edge of the table. " Get up, you lazy swine, you'll have time to sleep at home ! " The baton broke with the force of one blow. Furiously the policeman brought his fist down again.

Those who were being flogged, howled like wild beasts. The smell of sweat and leather filled the guardroom. The police warmed to it. With the constriction of their helmet-straps their blood pressure increased alarmingly.

Her body bent with pain, paralysed with excitement and terror, Anna stood at the door. Her eyes burnt in her head like two red-hot balls : her face was white as chalk. With trembling hands she held a shawl across her breast. Her fair hair hung in disorder over her forehead.

" Ha, ha, ha ! "

The police roared with laughter when they saw the young woman standing there in deadly fear. "We'll have some fun with her. She's pretty, the cow!"

"Come here, my precious. You'll get all you want here!" One of them pushed her to the front.

Some of the workers turned slowly round. "Faces to the walls, hands up!" shouted the policemen. But one of them, a young worker, could not take his eyes off. He was the only Communist among the arrested and he knew that this was the wife of Comrade Zimmermann. His face darkened. His nails cut deeply into the palms of his hands. And then suddenly he shouted as loud as he could: "You murderers—you swine—cowardly curs—if we only had arms!" He could not have kept silent any longer. He did not care what happened now. He had thrown his accusation into the midst of these grinning, mocking, brutal faces. Up here with the unarmed prisoners they were heroes, but what about the streets below? Down there they were filled with mortal terror of the fists of the proletarians; down there, they fired indiscriminately at anyone who showed himself. Brutes that had never had a drop of worker's sweat on their hands!

His furious screaming voice was stifled with a hail of blows. With a roar, seven or eight policemen fell upon him.

"Bloody Communist swine! Shut up!"

"Beat the pig to death!"

"We'll show you!"

They pushed each other out of the way to get in their blows. He fell to the ground, trying in vain to protect his head with his hands.

He was still screaming. They tramped on his face, kicked him in the open, screaming mouth. They continued to beat him with their rifles until he had lost consciousness.

Gasping they turned at last. Some of them were foaming at the mouth. "Now—that sod—is finished—the swine!"

They were speechless with excitement. But presently they turned to tidying their ruffled uniforms. An electric lamp hanging from the ceiling swung to and fro. The light flickered over the group of prisoners huddled together in the corner.

Anna had taken refuge behind a table and stared fascinated at the young man who lay motionless and face downward on the floor. Through his thick hair trickled slowly a dark stream which ran down the back of his neck to the dirty wooden boards. She had seen him once or twice together with Kurt, who liked this quiet, reliable young comrade.

" Well, you swine, now you have seen —that's what we'll do with all of you. We'll teach you to celebrate the first of May ! " Anna looked up in affright at the distorted face of the young policeman. His eyes were bulging out of their sockets. The leather strap pushed his brutal chin forward. His broad, muscular hand hung down with open fingers. Under the short, dirty, bitten nails the red lumps of flesh were curved upwards. And between his fingers there were stains of blood. Anna knew no more. Her anxiety for the child, for Kurt had completely disappeared. She merely gazed as if paralyzed at this muscular hand covered with red blood, the blood of the young worker. Her feverish brain hammered unceasingly . . . murderer's hand . . . murderer's hand . . . murderer's hand——

Perhaps she had gone mad already.

CHAPTER IX

THE SECOND NIGHT

ELEVEN O'CLOCK.
The streets about the alley were empty. Pitch
black the starless sky stretched above the houses
and yards. A tramcar with extinguished lights stood in the
Reinickendorferstrasse. Here and there shadows moved in
front of the houses. They moved noiselessly and were lost
again in the darkness. In a side street, two or three shots
broke the silence. Then all was quiet again.

The red spot of a cigarette glowed in one of the doorways
and revealed for a few seconds the yellow, unshaven face
of a worker, an advance guard of the alley. The headlights
of a private car moved stealthily along the pavement. The
car moved slowly, hesitatingly, its tyres crushed on some
broken glass. As if suddenly frightened, it stopped. The
electric light inside was extinguished. It turned and
dashed back at full speed from the unknown, from the
uncanny silence of the alley.

Such an impenetrable cover of blackness shrouded the
entrance to the alley, that it was invisible except to one
standing directly in front. By the shadowy outlines of an
overturned lorry burned the faint light of a red lantern.
Behind it was the black hole of the alley. No light in any
of the houses was to be seen, except that through cracks
in the damaged blinds of the " Red Nightingale " there was
a faint streak. A muffled hum of voices reached the street.
In the room at the back a meeting was being held.

Time was short ; they had to come to a quick decision.
Those who spoke about irrelevant matters were immediately
silenced. The more the resistance of the inhabitants grew,
the more obvious it became how fatally unprepared and
unorganized they were for this action.

150

"Armed insurrection," said some. "What with?" "With pop-guns and broomsticks?" replied others. "Do you perhaps want to start a civil war in Wedding?" "Of course, man, Thomas will become the red general and Hermann, People's Commissar of the Köslin quarter!"

Everybody laughed. Nervousness disappeared. They listened calmly. "Do you believe," said Hermann gravely, "that if the Party gave out the call for armed insurrection, we would remain armed with a few out-of-date pistols? Comrades, if that were the case, Berlin would look very different to-night! If to-day we defend ourselves against these bandits as best we can, that is not by any means a revolution, for a revolution very different conditions must exist. Economic mass struggles, political mass strikes, etc. But we have no time to speak of these matters at present."

The final decision was reached shortly before midnight when a courier brought the news that the police had again begun to cut off and surround the district. The lights were put out in the "Red Nightingale," the blind in front of the door was drawn up and through the narrow passage the workers pushed their way into the street.

Kurt stood with Hermann a few seconds longer, speaking softly about Anna. From the moment he had disarmed the policeman he had heard nothing more of her. Only just now in the "Red Nightingale" a woman had told him that Anna had been arrested and the boy taken home by a comrade. Someone had seen that she was beaten by the police. That was all. This uncertainty drove him half mad. He knew that she would not betray any secrets, but she might with the help of police witnesses be convicted of rebellion, violence or God knows what, and be sentenced to years of imprisonment.

It was with difficulty that Hermann stopped him from going to the police-station to search for her. Kurt was known as a Communist and they would simply have kept him there. Perhaps he would nevertheless have risked it, had he known when and how he would see her again.

. . . . . .

The noise of wooden beams being thrown into the street

alarmed the inhabitants. Doors banged. Some were running along in front of the houses. Someone called out of a window into the darkness whence the noises came. Paraffin candle and lights appeared on the landings. Women with lamps in their hands came down to the doors when they heard the men from the " Red Nightingale " working among the wood and iron tubes. When the first of them appeared carrying beams and long poles on their shoulders they understood what was happening. Within a few minutes everything was in full swing.

" Bring a light here ! " shouted a high-pitched voice. They could not see their own hands before their eyes. Through the darkness the unsteady, trembling lights shed their reflection on the men moving among the ruins of yesterday's barricades. Bright spots of light appeared in all the doorways and ran along the houses to the place of work.

Wood splintered. The door of the builder's hut flew open with a loud bang. The tools lying in readiness for the navvies were distributed. " Hi, what are you dreaming about—give us a hand ! " Pickaxes, spades and axes clashed on to the pavement. They took all the boards, sticks, etc. they could find lying about.

Hermann thought at first that they had all gone crazy ! When the procession of people carrying these things passed through the alley—between the grotesque shadows of the boards and poles, women were running with lamps—the boys suddenly started to sing, to sing loudly, as if they were demonstrating in the Lustgarten.

" For goodness' sake shut up ! You'll only set the police on our heels ! " Hermann shouted furiously. What did they mean by roaring the " International " now, in the middle of the night, in the silent, blockaded quarter, while in all probability the machine-guns of the police were posted a few hundred yards further on ?

But there was nothing doing ! As quickly as dried-up thirsty soil absorbs water, the melody was taken up by the people, by the whole alley. Women were hanging out of the black open windows, shouting and waving their hands.

They came running out of the doors, the pavements were suddenly filled with singing and laughing people. The dancing lights painted long moving shadows on the walls.

Hermann saw an old woman standing next to him who was carefully protecting the glass of her lamp from the wind with her hand, as if this were the most important thing in the world. Above it the face shone, a round white patch, in which the eyes looked out like two dark holes. The thin bloodless lips were moving with the song.

" Mad . . . quite mad ! " Hermann was thinking, but he meant something quite different.

Just before it reached the Wiesenstrasse the procession stopped. Picks and spades flew into action. Crash. Crash. The stones threw sparks. First they tore up the pavement to the right and left and lifted the heavy stone flags with crowbars.

" H-e-a-v-e—ho ! h-e-a-v-e—ho ! Look out comrades, mind your legs ! "

Crrrrash !

Three young workers appeared out of the darkness of the alley carrying a heavy gas street lamp on their shoulders.

" Look out, make room ! " Bang. The iron pipe fell across the road.

" Just bring a light here. Grete, come here." The women ran backwards and forwards with their lamps. Suddenly a short, muffled thud was heard from the Wiesenstrasse. A rocket rose.

" Lie down," someone shouted. For seconds the corner was lit up by a glaring green light. Trembling, long shadows ran over the houses as the ball of light sank to the ground. Hissing and smoking it fizzled out on the pavement just in front of the barricade. The police had sent out a patrol. Only the fear that the fire of their shots might show where they were prevented them from shooting.

Carefully three shadows moved in front of the barricade, closely pressed to the houses. Motionless they stood for a short period at the corner of the Wiesenstrasse, one with the grey of the wall. A hasty movement, just opposite a doorway, betrayed the police patrol through the silver buttons on their uniforms. The lights behind the barricade disappeared.

Peng . . . peng.

The window-panes in the entrance opposite fell to the ground in splinters. After a short but sharp exchange of shots, the police retreated. The work behind the barricade went on.

. . . . . .

Kurt returned to the alley with the other two comrades. He was slightly nervous. The police must have seen what was happening here. He exchanged a few words with Hermann and disappeared again into the dark.

Below, outside the " Red Nightingale " all was quiet. Yards of pavement had been torn up at the end of the alley, the road was strewn with large stones. It would be very difficult for any car to pass here. The guards had noticed nothing to arouse their suspicion. Carefully he went on. Some women were standing in a passage and talking in subdued voices. They did not recognise him until he was straight in front of them. No,—here too everything was all right.

It was dark and quiet in the Reinickendorfer-strasse. A taxi-cab came rattling up the street from the Nettelbeck-platz. Just before it reached the Weddingstrasse, its head-lights were switched on and lit up the street. A call from the other side of the street brought the car to a stop. But the lights continued to shine. Only when a stone had smashed the windscreen were they switched off ; the driver accelerated and disappeared at top speed.

Kurt whistled through his teeth. Damned mess. That car had not come here by accident. Were the police stationed at the Nettelbeckplatz ? He ran back as quickly as he could.

CHAPTER X

SHOCK TROOP G

FROM the darkened passage of police-station 95, steel helmets emerged. Twenty, thirty. The low iron rim almost hid the young faces beneath it.

A glowing cigarette end was flung to the ground, the wind blew sparks into the impenetrable darkness which swallowed the men. Carbines and bayonets rattled softly. A straight line of shadows only broken by the shining buttons on the uniforms, moved almost inaudibly, close along the houses till it reached the bridge. Behind the obtuse angle of the street corner was the Wiesenstrasse. Here they waited. A small, broadly built figure in a tight-fitting uniform moved away from the wall and noiselessly stepped forward a few paces.

In front of the officer the broad Wiesenstrasse lay dark and empty. On the left-hand side, about half-way down, was a dark gap—the alley! Only towards its lower end were tiny lights shining, their miserable glow was absorbed by the darkness at arms' length. From time to time the wind brought a muffled noise. From beneath the steel helmet a pair of night-glasses searched roofs and houses. But in vain. Houses and sky were one smooth, impenetrable wall.

Behind him was deadly silence. The men stood far back in the shadow of the porches. The silent darkness was uncanny. These empty streets, the black holes of the windows (you could not tell if they were open or closed) the yards and the alley tenements which lay deep in the shadow behind the bridge.

For the first time hand-grenades were hanging from their belts. With every movement they felt the wooden handles touch their bellies.

155

The officer returned. A few short, whispered commands. The carbines were cocked with a soft clink of metal.

" Extend the line ! "

The first five had hung their carbines round their necks. The fifth to the left was Sergeant Schlopsnies. The hands of the young policeman—otherwise so steady—were trembling when he screwed the safety pin from the hand-grenade. The little china ball on the end of a string, through which the explosion is caused, fell out and swung between his nervous fingers. He was trembling so violently that he feared to touch it. His whole body shook. Someone bumped into him by mistake in the dark. He was startled. A bullet pouch fell to the ground with a rattling noise. The officer raging with fury, suppressed a curse. In the dark gap on the left side of the street the lights suddenly went out. " Cursed fool ! There, see what you have done." The officer tore out his revolver. His highly pitched, sharp voice cut into the silence.

" Fire."

Crash—a carbine fusillade whipped into the gap.

" Attack.—Forward ! Forward ! "

Shouting they ran with wide open mouths straight into the black wall. " Ho—Ho—o—o ! Close the windows ! "

Schlopsnies tore at the string—his helmet knocked against someone—he stumbled roaring with fear—the hand-grenade slipped from his fingers—he ran on without thinking. A few yards behind him the bursting bomb tore up the pavement. A hailstorm of dirt and bits of stones fell over him.

At the entrance to the alley the deafening explosions of the hand-grenades flared up. The alley, the walls, the roofs, the whole uncanny night had suddenly come to life. Stones crashed on the pavement, revolvers spat fire. Immediately in front of Schlopsnies fell a heavy iron object. He had felt the wind of it as it passed his head. He tried to look up. That cursed helmet—one could see or hear nothing from underneath it. Perhaps they are throwing things from the roof ? He ran close to the houses for cover. A long-drawn howl pierced the night from the dark

hole of the alley . . . peng . . . peng . . . tak-tak-tak-tak
. . . the machine pistols shattered the human sound. Once
he heard the officer's voice a long way off. Now Schlopsnies
could see no one. He was choked with fear—he was alone,
alone in this hell outside the alley. Senselessly he potted
at the windows of the houses opposite. A shadow ran close
past him. Back?

A log fell with a hollow sound on the pavement, spewed
out by the night. More figures were running past him.
Policemen? Reds? He shouted after them. No one
heard. His feet were glued to the ground. He could not
run. Shots and explosions roared in his ears. A stone
struck his helmet and bounced off with a bang. "Hey,
hey, haaaalt!" he shouted. He stumbled across the street.
"I have a bullet in my head—right in the head—all is
smashed—finished. . . ."

.   .   .   .   .   .

From the bridge came the whistle of the officer twice in
quick succession. The men ran back in short, quick jumps
and gathered behind the corner. The attack had failed.

.   .   .   .   .   .

The people on the narrow stairs made room as someone
was carried up. A woman switched on an electric torch.
One man had taken the wounded under the arms; two
others held the feet.

"Owww . . . ugh . . . ow . . . !"

The soft groan echoed through the house. Hermann
stood on the landing of the first floor and opened the door
of his flat. Several were lying there already.

For a few seconds the light of the lamp lit up the silent,
frightened faces of the women standing there.

"It's little Otto," one of them whispered after the door
had closed.

Hermann quickly pushed the table under the lamp, and
carefully they lifted the victim. One placed a pillow under
his head. Now they could inspect the wound properly.
The lower part of one trouser leg was reduced to a blood-
stained rag.

Dum-dum bullet! thought Hermann biting his lips.

The ankle was completely shot to pieces! He tore a few linen sheets from the cupboard. The bandages had been used up long ago. While they tried to bind up as well as they could the pieces of flesh and splintered bone, a young woman stroked Otto's chalk-white, grimy face. Once she bent back her hands, she was trembling so.

No one knew this young woman worker. She was not from the alley. But Hermann remembered having seen her several times during the night trying to help in looking after the children and later the wounded. Kurt told him later that it was a young Social Democratic tobacco worker from Manolis, whom he had seen talking to a young comrade on the Nettelbeckplatz. . . .

.   .   .   .   .

Shortly before 4 o'clock the decisive attack was made. Eight closed taxis drove at great speed one behind the other straight up to the barricades. The guards near the Nettelbeckplatz had allowed the taxis to pass in good faith.

Before the workers on the barricades could take cover policemen in plain clothes jumped out of the cars and opened a furious fire on the alley. They drove forward at the point of the revolver the thirteen workers who had fallen into their hands, and compelled them to tear down the barricades. The prisoners were used as cover against the shots of the workers. During the first attack, Kurt had a small revolver—a mere toy in his large hands. Nevertheless he had felt he was not left completely helpless. Now, when he put his hand in his pocket he discovered to his despair that he had lost it when carrying rafters for the barricades. There was no possibility of replacing it. All the swearing in the world would not help. But at any rate he could put up a bluff—" And that gang," he thought " is terrified even of bangs." So he knelt down in the middle of the empty street and taking a pile of incendiary caps from his pocket placed one after the other carefully on a fig-stone.

Peng . . . it made quite a nice bang! The next one— peng . . . ! He was soon an expert in detonating the cap by hitting it with a small stone. Now he placed three or four of the small copper things together. BANG! That sounded like something real.

Sssss . . . t pfffee . . . ff bonc! The bullets of the police whistled around his ears. They took the flashes of the caps for shots and fired furiously in his direction. Lead squirted on to the pavements right and left, but Kurt sat by himself in the middle of the alley and let off caps. It was like a fair. The more they shot, the wilder he became. The alley was such a pitch black hole that he could only be hit by sheer accident. He did not notice that he had black wounds of burns on both of his hands. He noticed nothing else but that it banged whenever he hit. The main thing was to bang, as long as he went on banging the swine wouldn't dare to enter the alley. If the police should succeed in getting a firm stand at the entrance of the alley now, all would be lost, not a soul would escape from the mouse trap.

After a quarter of an hour the police withdrew with their prisoners from the half-destroyed barricade, but only so far that they could still keep the alley under fire from the surrounding houses of the Wiesenstrasse. Machine pistols hammered at every shadow that moved behind the barricade.

The most important position of the workers had thus been lost without resistance through this cunning manœuvre.

. . . . . .

Kurt felt his way through the dark passage to the stairs. Suddenly his hand came in contact with the warm soft face of a girl shrinking from his touch. The unexpected contact affected them both with a curious hostile sensation. In the midst of this cold solitude there was suddenly the warm closeness of a human body—a body, generalized, without individuality—it did not matter whose it was— but for the fraction of a second this sensation begot a fleeting sadness, which at the same time wakened the senses.

At this moment, Kurt saw the coming events of to-morrow for the first time calmly and relentlessly. He had been too much in the middle of the fighting to have any other desire than that of a machine-gun and an unending bullet belt. He had entirely forgotten the significance of the political starting point of these events. But now everything returned —and with inescapable clarity.

For a quarter of an hour everything had been at a standstill. The alley outside was silent and deserted and in darkness. Not a footstep was to be heard, not a door creaked. Silent and invisible faces gazed everywhere into the darkness ; on landings and stairs the people stood — and waited. It was as if a human being suddenly holds his breath for fear of not hearing something. But all was quiet, unbearably quiet. If only they would begin shooting again.

" They won't return before daybreak," the girl said calmly as she leaned back against the wall.

" Of course they will."

Kurt was still standing in front of her without either being able to see the other. It was soothing to hear this calm somewhat deep voice. For a moment he had almost believed that it was Anna he had touched. Who could tell where she was at this moment ? It was extraordinary how little he was concerned about it now. Perhaps he would have been more anxious if she had stayed in the alley. For those outside everything was finished—one way or the other. The girl's voice was vaguely familiar. He was too tired to think more about it. It was of no importance.

On the landing above them a door opened and subdued voices were heard. Then slow, careful steps moved down the stairs as if they were carrying someone.

" That will be Otto," the girl said. " His mother does not know anything yet. She was told he had been sent out as a courier."

A torchlight flashed through the passage and shortly afterwards a stretcher was carried round the corner. As they crossed the yard towards the back door leading to the Panke, a window was opened. Someone leaned out and then closed it again, since it was too dark to see anything. The bearers of the wounded disappeared noiselessly through the back-yards. Stretcher-bearing had gone on all night.

" See that you get away yourself somewhere through the back-yards there," Kurt said to the girl. He got no answer—she had gone. Curious. He did not even know whom he had spoken to.

CHAPTER XI

DAWN . . .

"BERGEN, why haven't those reports arrived yet?"
"It is only ten minutes to six, sir." As he answered the Police President, the official was trying with difficulty to sit straight in his chair. A number of telephones were standing in front of him. They were directly connected with the police headquarters on the Alexanderplatz.

The large, comfortably furnished room, in which the President continued his uneasy pacing up and down the carpet, was filled with the strange atmosphere of a sleepless night, intensified to an unbearable extent by the tension of a helpless, isolated uncertainty. He had paused repeatedly at the door and listened to subdued voices of the guards who had been stationed for the last few days in his villa in Zehlendorf. He would have loved to put on the wireless or play the gramophone if only to have some noise to break the unbearable silence and to shorten the night.

The official in the armchair was asleep again.

Half an hour earlier the Ministry of the Interior telephoned for the third time during the night offering the help of the Reichswehr troops who were standing in readiness, but he had refused it. The Police Commander had promised him shortly after midnight that all resistance would be crushed by the dawn of May 3rd. Ten minutes later the Commander's car had left the President's villa with full powers for unhampered action and up to now not a single intelligible report had come through from the Alexanderplatz. Would it not have been better if he had run across himself? But the Commander had been dead against it!

Nervously he put down his cigar. Evidently he could not stand the heavy tobacco any longer.

" Berger—what is the time ? "

The official jumped. " Two minutes to six, sir." After a pause he added : " Perhaps some black coffee would do you good, sir ? " He made a slight bow in his chair towards his chief as he said it. When he observed that the President did not take the slightest notice, he leant back again in his chair. " If all goes well," he was thinking, " I shall perhaps get two days additional leave. But, by God I wouldn't like to be in his skin ! What he must feel like—a fine Social Democrat ! " His thoughts became confused again.

The thick-set figure of the President was standing at the window. He pushed the velvet curtain aside. The first cold, grey-blue light of dawn came in the high window and mingled with the yellow rays of the electric chandelier, producing an unpleasant dead light.

Outside the wrought-iron gates the President saw the dew-moistened helmets of the police on guard. They were kicking their heels to keep warm. Behind the dew-laden gardens of the quiet suburb a grey streak appeared on the horizon. The third of May !

The fat, perspiring face drooped with a soft sound against the cool windowpane. The hours of inactive waiting had eaten into the bull-like brutality of the former metal worker like a devouring acid.

In the pale light of dawn, the flabby face of the President with its expressionless, glassy gaze, was frozen to a distorted yellow mask.

.   .   .   .   .   .

The telephone rang.

The official jumped up and took the receiver.

" Hallo. Hallo. Yes. The President's room. Yes. Speaking. Yes. Yes. At once ! " The official turned, receiver in hand :

" Northern district group command on the line, sir— action commenced five minutes ago ! "

The tired face of the President relaxed—he smiled.

.   .   .   .   .   .

Grete took two and three steps at a time as she dashed down the stairs in number 3. Close behind her was the dark-haired factory girl from Manolis'. Doors slammed and were bolted from the inside. An iron pail rolled noisily down the steps and was left lying in a corner. From the alley the heavy noise of an armoured car shook the house.

Tak . . . tak . . . tak . . . tak . . . rrrrrrtak . . . The short, sharp bark of a machine-gun. Plaster and dust fell from the dirty grey walls of the passage. A third person came out of a door which slammed behind him and stumbled heavily downstairs behind the two girls. It was still dark on the narrow stairs.

The front door was torn open just as Grete had reached the last step in her attempt to escape through the passage at the back. In the grey light of the morning stood the sharp silhouette of a man with rumpled, disordered hair. The left arm hung stiffly down, black moisture trickled over his hand. The paper boy of the *Vorwärts* had been fired at by the police.

Through the half-open door, Grete heard an officer's loud voice. Steel helmets and uniform buttons glittered out of a cloud of morning mist and powdery smoke. A policeman rushed past with raised carbine. The alley swarmed with men roaring and firing. The door banged to and swallowed the momentary view of the alley. The tobacco girl was trying to lift the heavy iron bar into position.

Butt ends thundered against the door.

" Open—or we shoot ! " someone shouted from outside. " Quickly. See that you get away," she whispered terrified, while she still tried to push the iron further into the hooks which at present only held the edge of the bar. Grete tore the wounded man with her across the yard, thinking that the girl was following.

With a superhuman effort the girl hung with her whole weight on the iron bar. Her small trembling body was pressed against the timber shaken by the blows which the police rained on to the door from the outside. Only hold on, was her sole thought, otherwise the other two are lost !

Her head was thrown against the hard wood by a terrible blow from outside. Stunned she fell backward. Her hands slowly slipped from the bar. The beating and shooting became merged in her ears in a gurgling roar. With a metallic clank the bar jumped from the hook—the door was open.

She staggered trying in vain now to escape towards the yard. Peng—her hands with stretched fingers flew into the air, her knees gave way and then she fell without a sound on her face in the middle of the passage.

Passage and yard were occupied, the searching of the houses for arms began. For hours the young, dark-haired tobacco girl lay amidst blood and dirt on the grey stone floor. The police might have thought she was dead, they did not allow anyone to come near. Once one of the attackers went over to her, bent down and picked up a moist shred of a garment from her back with the tip of his finger. Her back was a black, wet pulp of blood, flesh and pieces of cloth.

" 'Strewth—it's effective at short distances ! " he said to one of his mates and dropped the rag again. A few hours later the tobacco worker—Sophie Herder—was dead.

.   .   .   .   .   .

House after house was occupied, flats searched, cupboards torn open, children dragged out of their beds, mattresses thrown on to the floor. Where were the Reds ? Where were their arms ? The women stood in the flats, arms akimbo next to the policemen, and held their tongues. Not a word was to be got out of them.

" Find your ' sharp-shooters ' yourselves if you want them ! "

" Where is your husband ? "

" How should I know, I'm not his wet nurse ! "

" Have you arms in this flat ? "

" Of course . . . knife and fork, and a cooking pot too ! "

" Damned vermin ! "

Beside the armoured car which had stopped outside number 6 there stood the Deputy G. with his great black hat on, protesting against the arbitrary arrests. His presence protected the arrested from being manhandled, there and then on the street. Indiscriminately the police arrested all who fell into their hands. Should Berlin be treated to the farce of a handful of proletarians keeping thousands of policemen, equipped with the most modern weapons at bay for three days ?

"The gang is still inside, sir. We'll get 'em out—you bet your life," shouted the officer to the deputy and then dashed furiously into the next house.

Kurt knew the alley with its yards and passages, like the back of his hand. He dodged from house to house. Whenever he saw that a house was going to be searched he escaped one way or another into the next. He heard the voice of the officer in charge and was barely in time to cross the yard and jump from the dustbin over the wall. As he landed the bullets of the officer covered him in a cloud of plaster and dust.

They had seen him this time ; in a few seconds this house would be searched, too. He knew what to expect if they got hold of him. In the Ufer station they knew him only too well.

In a few leaps he had reached the stairs to the cellar, one bound down the steps. To the left there lived a sympa-thiser, to the right there was a low door, scarcely visible to anyone who did not know the place. He already heard the sound of the nailed boots running across the yard. He pushed some rubbish which lay about there in front of the cellar door and softly closed it behind him. "I am either saved or trapped ! " he thought.

He started. Something had moved. In the dark, narrow hole which had only a small window with a broken pane, he had a feeling that he was not alone. Two of them, with drawn breath, waited each for the other. Slowly Kurt grew accustomed to the darkness. In the corner lay a dark motionless mass.

They were shooting in the yard. A window splintered and crashed on the stones below. The light was obscured as someone paused in front of the cellar window.

"The swine must still be somewhere round about," a

policeman called out. Steps descended the cellar stairs. Kurt was still standing closely pressed to the low door and heard the panting of the policemen outside. The black lump in the corner remained motionless.

Someone kicked the door of the cellar dwelling opposite "Hi! Open! Police!"

A cursing woman's voice replied, then the door creaked. "What do you want. There's no one here. My husband is in the hall!"

They even moved the furniture from the wall. Cursing they went upstairs again five minutes later.

"Great luck that time, what?" the lump whispered after a while. It was a homeless man who had settled down in this hole. If they had caught him, he would have been dealt with as a "rioter" like all the rest.

They were still firing outside. For the moment Kurt was saved. He sat on an empty box and buried his tired face in his hands. Where was Hermann? Where was Anna? And the girl from the passage last night? Where were all the others? Escaped in time or perhaps already in the hands of the police. What of Anna? What was happening outside? Why are they still shooting—and *whom*? And then, what would happen next? All this cannot simply pass over. To-morrow the papers will scream their lies again. To-morrow? Of course. To-morrow he would have to go back to his job again, to carry cement. Will the workers of Berlin simply remain silent? One must start at once, wake them up, inform them, tell them how it all happened. All those Social Democrat workers! Old Tölle on the job. What will he say to all this?

He felt that he would choke in this depressing cellar. He had to escape.

"Are you mad?" the other said, "where on earth are you going?"

"To look for the comrades!" was Kurt's simple reply when he pushed back the cellar door.

CHAPTER XII

"THE POLICE PRESIDENT WISHES IT TO BE MADE KNOWN . . ."

4th May, 1929 (Police Report).

" On Friday and Saturday night the following persons were taken in seriously wounded condition to the municipal hospitals where they died later : Hermann Langenderger, aged 25, address unknown, shot in the chest ; Ernst Masloch, aged 20, address unknown, shot in the stomach ; Martin Baledowski, aged 21, Harzerstrasse 2, shot in the chest ; Charl. Makay, correspondent of the *Waitara Daily*, New Zealand, aged 46, shot in the stomach. These persons died in Buckow Hospital. In addition, Otto Engel, aged 19, Ackerstrasse 45, shot in the stomach, died in the Virchow Hospital ; and Walter Bath, Neukölln, Wehnerstrasse 37, shot in the stomach, in the Urban Hospital.

" In addition, three persons were killed on the spot. The hospitals and municipal first-aid stations have taken in 29 wounded persons. The number of those killed has thus reached 25."

3rd May, 1929 (*Vorwärts*).

" The Police President wishes it to be made known : The Police President has prohibited the publication of the newspapers *Die Rote Fahne* and *Das Volksecho* for infringement of paragraph 7, sections 4 and 21, for a period of three weeks, until May 23rd, inclusive. These papers have given active support to the attempts of the Communist part of Germany to undermine the constitutional republican status of the Reich."

4th May, 1929 (*Hamburger Nachrichten*).

" We may remind our readers of the words of Napoleon that each rebel killed means 100,000 citizens saved. If instead of several hundred arrests and only a few (!) killed, the proportion had been the reverse, then the middle classes could have had confidence in the present government. . . ."

4th May, 1929 (*Vorwärts*).

" SPRING'S AWAKENING.

" . . . the days of love, of beauty, of sweet scents have commenced. Blessed are we who are full of happiness, full of thanksgiving, full of hope and expectation.

" Pan, joyous God of Life, accept our gratitude that you have placed in contrast to ourselves, as a warning to us, the dried-up old souls of monks and ascetics with their songs frozen on their lips for thousands of years, in the barren desert. With gracious smiles the dance of true life whirls around them, in white and red blossom, light and dark eye, in purple cheek and luxurious lip.

" Spring's awakening, song of infinite delight, ocean of limitless bliss ! Jubilant I throw myself into your blue waters. Let them close above me.

HEINRICH BRÄM."

4th May, 1929 (Special Report).

" In order to pacify the centres of unrest, Wedding and Neukölln, in which grave fighting again took place yesterday evening and in the course of the night, I have ordered the following measures to be taken :

" Between the hours of 9 p.m. and 4 a.m. all traffic in the streets mentioned below is prohibited. Exceptions are made only in the case of doctors, midwives and ambulance-men. There must be no loitering on doorsteps in porchways and corners. The windows giving on the streets must remain closed during the hours mentioned. Nor must there be any light in rooms facing the street during these hours. Inhabitants infringing these orders expose themselves to risk of having their windows fired on by the police.

" During the daytime no person is allowed to linger in the districts and streets mentioned, or on house-landings, corners, or entrances. The police have special orders to see that no one remains longer on the streets than is absolutely necessary. Persons moving on the streets without a definite place of destination will be arrested. Three or more persons must not walk together. All cycling is prohibited. Public houses and restaurants situated within the districts mentioned will be closed at 9 p.m.

" Persons infringing these rules will endanger their lives.

The Police President,
(*Signed*) ZÖRGIEBEL."
(*Seal.*)

5th May, 1929 (*Volkszeitung*—Mosse).

" . . . the ' special measures ' enforced yesterday by the Police President seem to have caused a blind mania for shooting by the police, and this mad raging of the police war machine let loose on the inhabitants has become—we cannot, unfortunately resist this conclusion—a public menace. Things cannot possibly continue as they are at present. . . ."

6th May, 1929 (Police Report).

" The Police President wishes it to be made known :

" . . . My warning not to enter the danger zone and my advice that any person not following the measures taken will endanger his life, have been disregarded by several persons who have suffered as a consequence. . . . It has not been established from which side the fatal shot was fired. . . ."

6th May (W.T.B. Report).

" The Berlin public prosecutors have decided to confiscate the bodies of those killed during the May Day celebrations and to allow their burial only after the official post-mortem examination. These examinations are to take place within the next few days.

" The examinations will be made in the presence of the local magistrates of Neukölln and Berlin-Wedding by two doctors, one of whom will be a police-court doctor."

.   .   .   .

14th May, 1929.

Deposition of :

" Paul Walsowsky, compositor, accompanied by his wife Jenny, aged 54 and 49 respectively, domiciled at Berlin SO 36, Harzerstrasse 2, second floor, front, identified through tram season ticket, member of the S.P.D. and of the Verband der Deutschen Buchdrucker (Printers T.U.), who makes the following statement, being prepared to repeat it on oath :

" ' My wife is a member of the Frauenhilfe Martin Luther II in Neukölln (women's club organized by the church). The club had arranged a spring festival for the 3rd May, 1929 at 7 p.m. in Kliens Festsäle, which was however cancelled by the chairman, Rev. Leist, at the request of the police. Instead, we two therefore went with two other families to the Ashinger Café on the Kaiser-Friedrich-Platz in Neukölln. When we returned to our flat about 11 o'clock, our twenty-year-old son Martin was, to our surprise, missing from home. Early next morning we heard to our horror that our son Martin had been shot by the police (shot in the back). Further details of how and where this happened have not been given to us. We only know from the doctor in attendance at the Erckstrasse Neukölln first aid station, that our son was taken there dead by four men in a taxi-cab at 9.55 p.m. On the 4th May, 1929, the next day, we entered our flat between 3 and 5 p.m. and found a note signed by a police sergeant, informing us that our son was in the Neukölln Hospital. He was buried from there on Saturday 11.5 (Jacobi Cemetery).

" ' I wish to add that the doctor at the first-aid station in the Erckstrasse informed me when giving particulars of his examination after my son had been brought to him, that even a funeral procession had been shot at in the Mainzerstrasse in Neukölln.

" ' We have received the papers of our son, but not the key and purse of money which he took with him when he left the house.

" ' From my own observation I would like to add the following :

" ' About 6.30 p.m. I saw how two policemen who were on a lorry in the Friedrichstrasse in Neukölln struck a passing cyclist who wore a red carnation in his buttonhole, with their fist in the back of the neck, although the latter had not given the slightest cause for such action.'

> Berlin, 14th May, 1929.
> V. G. U.,
>> (*Signed*) PAUL WALDOWSKY,
>> JENNY WALDOWSKY *née* RENFAND."

The Prussian Minister of the Interior, II, 1420, V.

> Berlin, 3rd May, 1929.

To the Secretariat of the R.F.B.

Deed.   *Enactment.*

" In accordance with par. 14 and with par. 7 of the Protection of the Republic Act of July 21st, 1922 2nd June, 1927 (R.G.Bl.. I, p. 585, p.125) and in accordance with the Decree ruling the execution of this Act, dated 12th February, 1926 (R.G.Bl., I, p. 100) and in accordance with par. 2 of the National Law on Associations of April 19th, 1908 (R.G.Bl., p. 151) in connection with par. 129 of the National Decree of Penalties, the Rote Frontkämpferbund E. V. including the Rote Jungfront and the Rote Marine with all its institutions, is hereby dissolved within the boundaries of the Prussian Free State, with the consent of the government of the Reich (Severing, Müller, Hilferding and Wissell)* ;   because its activities show that its purpose is in conflict with the legal enactments above mentioned.

* All leaders of the S.P.D.

" The property of the organisations named above will be confiscated by the Reich in accordance with par. 18 of the Protection of the Republic Act and par. 3 of the Act of March 22nd, 1921.

" The confiscations will be carried out by the local police authorities.

(Signed) GRZESINSKI."

(Seal.)

On May 12th the secretariat of North subdistrict of the Communist Party of Germany was informed that the Köslinerstrasse cell had during the preceding week accepted 180 people living in the alley as new members of the Communist Party. The five brothers of the worker Schäfer who was shot by the police have also joined the Party and took a solemn oath of revenge at their brother's graveside. The alley was decorated by the inhabitants with flags draped with mourning crepe.

Va S. Reg. 903/29, Nr. 1,
   zu B. I., 759/29,
     Press material.

Dresden, 13th May, 1929.

DECREE.

" In the proceedings against the unknown author of the pamphlet ' Bloody May-days in Berlin,' issued by Werner Hirsch, Internationaler Arbeiterverlag, Berlin, for high treason and endangering the public peace, the application of the Dresden public prosecutor for confiscation of the pamphlet mentioned is hereby conceded.

" The contents of the pamphlet mentioned, the distribution of which is for payment and, in certain instances, free of charge, more or less openly incites for a violent change in the constitution of the German Reich and different classes of the population are incited to commit violence against one another—in a manner which endangers the public peace.

" Thus on page 27 :

" ' Zörgiebel acted upon the instructions of Social Democracy. Zörgiebel's crime was not an individual crime. However much this man who, like Noske, seems to represent the old-time type of the Prussian sergeant, and was qualified for his rôle of bloodhound by his unscrupulous brutality as well as his coarse and narrow-minded ignorance —the question of the workers' blood spilt during these Berlin May days can never be merely regarded as a question for Zörgiebel, alone.'

" Page 28 :

" ' The S.P.D. wanted bloodshed.'

" Page 29 :

" ' The Communist Party of Germany and armed insurrection : the Communists have no need to hide their plans and intentions. The Communist Party is a revolutionary party and does not deny that its aim is the overthrow of the capitalist system and the establishment of the dictatorship of the proletariat as the necessary pre-condition for socialism.'

" Crime according to par. 81, section 2 R. St. G. B. and par. 86 R. St. G. B.

" Inasmuch as the pamphlet serves as proof of the crime envisaged in the Act and as such is subject to confiscation, confiscation is justified (par. 94, and 98 R. St. G. B.).

High Court of Dresden, Abt. V.,

(*Signed*) BUSCH."

24th May, 1929 (Press report).

" The Berlin-Lankwitz branch of the Sozialistische Arbeiterjugend (Youth Organisation, S.P.D.) accepted a resolution of protest against expulsion, enforced by the party leaders, of the former S.P.D. party member Otto Mücke, who participated in May Day demonstrations. The resolution contains the following sentences : ' We approve of the participation of our group leaders and of the party delegate in the May Day demonstration. The campaign of denunciation against the demonstrators which fills the S.P.D. press since the bloody events of May 1st is equally directed against us. We do not regard the ban of the demonstration as an exceptional measure; on the contrary, we recognise it as an additional proof for the fact that the S.P.D. leadership acts less and less in the interests of the workers, but more and more in the interests of the capitalists. We regard this development of the S.P.D. with indignation and hereby resign from the S.A.J.' "

Bochum, 24th May. (*From our special correspondent.*)

" Hugo Dreckmann, member of the Werne City Council and for many years president of the local branch of the Social-Democratic Party, has sent his social-democrat membership book together with an application for membership of the Communist Party to the editor of the Communist paper *Ruhr Echo* ; he enclosed a letter in which he gives detailed political reasons for this step. Dreckmann has been a member of the Social Democratic Party since October 1st, 1904, that is for almost twenty-five years."

26th May, 1929 (*Vorwärts*) :

(Editorial.—On the opening of the Magdeburg S.P.D. Party Conference.)

" . . . Since dissatisfaction seems to be an inevitable feature of Social Democracy, there certainly will be, as there always has been, a good deal of criticism of the results of the Party's policy. But there is not the slightest suggestion among the rank and file of the Party that the cause of the workers could be defended more effectively by any other party, group or sect. No matter how great the wish may be that the Party be different in many respects than it appears to-day, all are united in the conviction that the Social Democratic Party, and only the Social Democratic Party is capable of leading the cause of the workers to victory.

FRIEDRICH STAMPFER."

26th May, 1929.

The Police President, Dept. IA.
   Tgb.-Nr. 458 IA 1/29.

To the Editor, *Die Rote Fahne*, Berlin C.25,
   Kleine Alexanderstrasse 28.

   " Enclosed you will find an endorsed copy of a letter which has been sent to-day to the publishers and the editor of *Die Rote Fahne* for your information.

                              (*Signed*) ZÖRGIEBEL."
              (*Endorsed*) PETERS, Pol. Kzl.-Assistant.
                                          (*Seal.*)

   " ' I hereby prohibit in accordance with par. 7 and par. 21 of the Protection of the Republic Act of July 21st, 1922 (Reichsgesetzblatt S. 585) the publication of the newspaper *Die Rote Fahne* and of its subsidiaries *Das Volksecho* and *Volkswacht* for a period of four weeks until June 22nd, inclusively. This prohibition covers any publication claimed to be a new one, which by its contents proves that it is the old paper. An appeal against this enactment is permissible within two weeks from the date of its receipt. The original appeal with two copies should be sent to me.'

REASONS :

   " The following passages occur in Nr. 104 of the *Rote Fahne* of May 25th, 1929, in the paragraph ' Legal or illegal —the fight goes on,' of the article ' Is Moscow to blame ? ' :
   " ' The Communist Party and the revolutionary proletariat have been strengthened by the struggles of May 1st. They did not allow themselves to be provoked to a decisive battle, but they took up the fight and will continue it with all means, legal or illegal. The Communist Party as the advance guard of the exploited and suppressed masses declares openly that the Zörgiebel murders of the days from May 1st to 3rd open a new stage in the class struggle, a stage in which the unscrupulous brutality of social fascism acting in the service of the capitalist system which is

condemned to death by history, rebounds against the iron determination and readiness for sacrifice of the working-class. The Communist Party declares plainly and openly that only the violent overthrow of the bourgeois state can put an end to all the terrors of the capitalist régime, of the exploitation of the millions, and to the horrors of the approaching imperialist war.'

" In the same number we read in the article ' The truth about the May-Day Bloodbath,' in the paragraph ' The workers of Berlin demonstrate ' :

" ' In reality it was just the heroic fighting discipline, the resolute resistance of the masses of workers which gave the first of May its characteristic appearance in spite of police terror. The police raged, batoned, turned on the fire-hose—the masses remained. The police cordons drove the assembled working men and women from one place to another with the brutality of sadistic cossacks, they rode their horses into masses and a few minutes later the masses stood there again, and again were in control of the street. The workers of Berlin have given triumphant proof of their heroism on this May 1st ! '

" These passages glorify the resistance of the Berlin workers to the decrees of the police presidium. They are a logical conclusion of the demands raised by the Communist Party prior to May 1st in the *Rote Fahne* and elsewhere, that the workers should on no account submit to the demonstration ban of 13*th February*, 1929, but, on the contrary, should break it by force.

" Demands such as these show that the Communist Party is an organisation inimical to the State in the sense of par. 129, St. G. B., because it is a part of its aims and business to prevent or nullify measures of the administration by illegal means, that is to say, by force. The argument that it is only possible to terminate all terrors of the capitalist régime by force, and the references to the exploitation of the millions and the horrors of the approaching imperialist war serve to undermine the constitutionally established republican form of the State, and further, to prepare the way for a violent overthrow of the constitution. The

Rote Fahne, by publishing these arguments of the Communist Party, whose central organ it is (*vide* heading of the paper) supports actively in its columns the aims of an organisation, inimical to the State, *viz.* the C.P.G. The conditions envisaged in par. 7 and par. 21 of the Protection of the Republic Act are therefore given. The prohibition is thus justified.

" The longest admissible term for the ban was assigned because although the paper was prohibited for the same reason from the 2nd to the 23rd of May, 1929, it has nevertheless continued its previous policy.

(*Signed*) ZÖRGIEBEL."

(Seal of the Police President.)

Witness : (Signature illegible).

CHAPTER XIII

END AND BEGINNING . . .

AS Kurt Zimmermann came home on the evening of
May 28th, he found the kitchen window dark, as it
always had been since May Day. But as he crossed
the dark yard, weary after his day's work, Hoffman's wife
called out to him. A letter had arrived, bearing a police
stamp on the cover. She had been told about it by the
postman who had known all the families in the alley for
years. It was too dark in the yard for her to notice the
sudden change in Kurt's face. He disappeared at once in
the low porch. The white globe of the gas-lamp in the
kitchen vibrated with the trembling of his hands.

A narrow official envelope sealed with a blue service
stamp. The front did not show the name of the sender.
He lifted the letter to the light—as if that would tell him
anything. He hesitated a few minutes longer ; then he
tore open the envelope :

Prison Hospital, Berlin, Lehrter Strasse,
    Tgb.-Nr. III /126 /29, Dept. IA.
              Berlin, May 27th, 1929.

      Herrn Kurt Zimmermann.
               Berlin N.,
               Köslinerstrasse, 6.

" In reply to your written enquiry, dated 6th May, 1929,
we beg to inform you that the arrested Anna Zimmermann
(*née* Berthold), of Berlin, N., Köslinerstrasse 6, is at
present in the prison hospital, Berlin, Lehrter Strasse,
Dept. G, room 4, bed 32.

" Applications for visitors' permits should be sent three days in advance to the Prison Governor, Berlin-Moabit, Lehrter Strasse.

" Prison-Hospital-Administration.

(*Signed*) HERMANN, Justizwachtmeister."

(*Seal.*)

When Hermann's wife who had looked after Kurt in these days, peered through the kitchen window an hour afterwards, she saw Kurt sitting at the table supporting his head in both hands and gazing blankly at the spot where the letter was lying.

. . . . .

Three days later.

Following a woman warder, Kurt entered a long room, lined right and left with rows of grey beds. The occupants —all women—were at once called to order if they raised their heads to look at the man. Kurt's eye strayed from face to face, was caught for a second by the bars of a window and then searched further. In one bed there lay a woman holding a dirty towel, wound in a thick knot like a baby in her arms. Her white face bore an expression of ecstatic happiness, she murmured soft words of endearment to the towel, while her hands caressed it with indescribable delicacy. The woman next to her coarsely winked at Kurt behind the back of the wardress and tapped her finger to her forehead while an ugly grin distorted her face. Behind him he heard a woman's laughter.

The wardress stopped at the last bed on the right.

" To-day for the first time she hasn't a temperature," she said to Kurt. " Otherwise you wouldn't have been let in. You have ten minutes."

Kurt did not hear what she was saying, he only saw the narrow, bloodless face on the pillow, with haggard protruding temples on which the blue veins seemed to be covered by a thin glaze. Out of dark rings below the forehead the eyes were staring at him, eyes in which there was something strange and new.

Was this—Anna ?

She was fully conscious for the first time to-day. For days and nights she had been in a raging fever. She had not the slightest idea how she had got here. Kurt held her thin, strangely dry hand carefully in his own, as if it were made of fragile china.

The wardress tried to interrupt their conversation several times. Anna started to talk about the people in the alley. She had read no papers. Only this morning a new patient in the room had told her what had happened in Berlin since her arrest. And also that a lawyer of the Party had seen to it that she was taken to the hospital. For the first time a faint smile lit up her face when she told Kurt that she had been charged with rebellion and resistance against the State authority.

" But, Anna, that is sheer madness."

" No, boy—I was very silly before. But why did you never tell me ? I too thought that it all had nothing to do with ' resistance against the authority of the State.' Do you know, at first I only went with the demonstration because I was afraid for you. And then—everything turned out different. I didn't know that the ' resistance ' against this authority, this State which I always considered to be something ' impartial,' something that was above party, is an essential part of the class struggle. Well, my boy, I have learnt that every fight of the workers for their rights, must be a fight against this State. When they beat little Willi almost to death in that police-station—Kurt, then I grasped what ' State authority ' means ! "

" You are not allowed to speak like this, Mrs. Zimmermann," the wardress interrupted her, but the tone of her voice was not unkind. Kurt noticed that she had listened silently and attentively. The ten minutes must have passed long ago, he thought.

" Let me go on," Anna said. " In front of the judge I shall say much more. I shall tell him that the people who to-day hold the power of the State in their hands are nothing but the deadly enemies of the workers, that they use the State power for nothing, but to protect the interests of the capitalists and to suppress the rights of the workers. And I shall tell the Social Democratic workers—I shall tell them in court—that their leaders who support this State are our enemies just as much, whom we must exterminate, if we want to live. I have learnt that on this year's first of May."

" Anna, you have not asked how our boy is getting on," Kurt said only to change her thoughts. Her pale face was already beginning to burn with the returning temperature.

" I have thought so much about him, but I thought more about the comrades. Most of them I only know by sight, I don't even know their names. Kurt, I am so ashamed that you have had such a bad comrade in me."

Kurt took both of her hands : " And now we shall have a very good and brave comrade ! Anna, we shall all be waiting for you. . . ."

He got up quietly when the wardress touched his shoulder. Anna lay with closed eyes. Above her head hung the chart with wild jumps in the temperature graph. She seemed asleep. The narrow mouth in the tired face bore a confident smile.

.   .   .   .   .   .

Vorwärts, November 5th, 1930.

" Comrade Zörgiebel who is now temporarily retiring from public life, but who, undoubtedly, will soon find a sphere of action giving full scope to his high merit and capacities, has gained the respect and sympathy of the widest circles of the Berlin population. Those who had the privilege of watching his work at close quarters know that a warm humanity and the desire to help have always been his leading aims. The gratitude and best wishes of all reasonable and decent inhabitants of Berlin will accompany him to his new activity."

THE END

THE RED ALLEY

The street came to life and roared
decked itself out with the bodies of men
set arms going, heads thinking,
mouths—rifles ; heads—crowbars.

Street : hard, inexorable
bowed backs
overweighted : the wheels and the footsteps
trundle their loads.

Hoist them up
Torn
Lacerated
pitiful bodies :
beat them down again
all the pained and oppressed—
Police stations, Police squadrons

Street of slavery
Street of Demonstration.

JOHANNES R. BECHER.